# HOLD ME CAPTIVE

by

MARGARET PARGETER

## Harlequin Books

TORONTO • LONDON • NEW YORK • AMSTERDAM • SYDNEY • WINNIPEG

Original hardcover edition published in 1976
by Mills & Boon Limited

ISBN 0-373-02022-8

Harlequin edition published November 1976
Second printing March 1977

Printed in Canada

# CHAPTER ONE

Amanda Trent had just had a bath. Relaxed and smelling sweetly of her favourite bath essence, she was anything but prepared for the sound of stealthy footsteps on the corridor outside. So far as she knew she was entirely alone in the flat. Head flung back, sapphire blue eyes startled, she listened. There was, along the corridor, a loose board which creaked when trodden on, and it was definitely creaking now!

'Is anyone there?' she called loudly, suddenly finding her voice, her frantic cry as she grabbed her white bathrobe a mixture of bewilderment and fear.

The lock on the bathroom door hadn't been entirely reliable for some time, but when two girls occupied a flat such a matter was not of paramount importance. Usually the tightly closed door was enough to indicate that the small room was occupied. In fact Amanda, since returning from America three weeks ago, had forgotten that the lock gave beneath the slightest push. And if she had remembered she would only have shrugged and said it didn't matter. The flat was leased, and the lease was not to be renewed. One faulty lock was neither here nor there. There was only her sister Veronica, and Veronica's new husband, Herman, and they would be the last people on earth to intrude.

To Amanda's dismay the footsteps drew nearer, halting abruptly directly outside the door. Nervously fascinated, quite unable to look away, she stared, now feeling trapped and utterly frightened. Veronica and Herman had not intended coming home for dinner this evening. They'd arranged to meet in the West End after work and have a meal out. Yet who else could it be but Veronica? She must have returned for something. It wasn't impossible. Amanda's mind reeled, clinging in thought to her sister.

No one had answered her short, sharp query, but surely it must be she who was there?

Only three months ago Veronica had married Herman Allen from the American Embassy. Veronica, at thirty-five, was fifteen years older than Amanda, and Herman was her second husband. Her first marriage had ended in divorce. Amanda's mother had died when she was born, leaving her to be brought up by a somewhat elderly relation who hadn't really cared very much. But since their father had married again when Amanda was sixteen she had lived with Veronica in this flat, apart from the time she had spent abroad.

During the last two years, while she had been away, Amanda had been almost too busy to acquire so much as a boy-friend, nevertheless she was happy for Veronica, even if she had reservations about Herman. In the short time she had known him she had found him amiable if somewhat lacking in purpose. Moreover, he had raised no objections when Veronica had asked that Amanda should be allowed to accompany them back to America. Veronica had pleaded and Amanda, until this moment, when the bathroom door jerked suddenly open, had been quite willing. But not now. Certainly not now!

Amanda knew it would be impossible as soon as Herman stepped over the threshold, a wide, facetious grin stuck on his over-smooth, over-cared-for face, looking very much like a fox trying to fool an unsuspecting chicken. Her momentary relief faded as the thought pierced sharply and she shivered in spite of the heat of the room, eyeing him warily, yet not willing, even at this stage, to jump to the wrong conclusions. There could be some simple explanation.

The bathrobe didn't cover her neatly. It caught and clung to one damp shoulder, for an instant exposing a whiteness of skin, a glimpse of enticing curves which were partly responsible for the sex-appeal she didn't know she possessed but which Herman was hard put to it to resist. One quick, impatient tug wrapped her safely within the ample

6

coverage of soft towelling, and her voice tinged with the same impatience, she asked shortly, 'Did you want something, Herman? I did shout, and you must have heard me?'

He was unperturbed; the facetious grin broadened into something slightly different. For a second he halted, his eyes lifting to Amanda's face, around which her short dark hair was a shining cap, his gaze lingering on the satiny texture of her cheeks, her eyes fringed with thick, silky lashes. That her sensitively shaped mouth with its short upper lip was in no way relaxed, he didn't appear to notice. 'Veronica is out,' he muttered thickly.

'Of course she is—you arranged to meet her, and you must know you shouldn't be here,' Amanda retorted sharply, all in one breath, while her senses, screaming in protest, flashed red. Apprehension tore along her nerves, yet she knew she must try to handle this with delicacy. Otherwise the whole silly thing could explode into a nightmare. Never had she experienced anything like this before, but there must be ways and means, if she kept her head. Staring at him coolly, she forced a slight smile. 'If you'll kindly remove yourself, Herman, I'll join you in a moment. Then, if there's anything I can do . . .?'

It seemed inevitable that her tactics failed. 'There's a whole lot you can do, honey!' He moved nearer, his eyes fixed on her figure, his tone heavily suggestive.

In fright, suddenly devastating, Amanda took notice of her built-in radar. She forgot about being tactful. Her voice rose an octave and came clearer. 'Herman, you're being ridiculous! I told you to wait outside.'

'And just supposing I don't want to?' Herman's fat lower lip stuck out stubbornly. 'You're quite a looker, honey. Sometimes I kind of wish I'd met you first, but we could still have fun.'

Disgust replaced temporarily Amanda's very real alarm as she stared disbelievingly at the man who stood before her. Had Herman taken leave of his senses? Wasn't he aware that Veronica got jealous? Surely, if he loved his wife, he wasn't mad enough to jeopardise their whole future, to say nothing of any future relationship between his wife and her sister! Veronica, if she ever learnt about this, would never believe Amanda had done nothing to encourage him. The taut pain of disillusionment caught Amanda and held her. Men, she decided irrationally, were all the same.

'One step nearer,' she said coldly, her blue eyes flashing, 'and I'll tell Veronica about this myself!'

'You must be joking!' There was a sharp little silence as, momentarily nonplussed, Herman halted. 'Oh, come on, honey, you've had no objections so far.' His eyes lingered greedily on the smooth curve of Amanda's throat, the vibrant paleness of her skin.

'What on earth do you mean?'

'Well . . . You must know what I mean, honey!' Herman's lips twisted smugly. 'Why, since you got back, you've trailed Veronica and me around. I kinda got the notion you were fond of me.'

'Fond of you!' Amanda choked on a wave of pure indignation. He had a nerve! 'Herman,' she said clearly, 'you're quite mistaken. I hadn't given it a thought, one way or another. I only went out with the two of you because you both insisted, and I thought Veronica would be hurt if I refused. I think I was beginning to like you, but don't get me wrong.'

'Honey,' Herman was smirking, 'I don't think I have, in spite of what you say. I'm an attractive man—a little younger than your sister.'

Amanda edged backwards, her hands behind her, praying and groping. This scene had all the makings of some cheap charade, and she might need something more solid than her wits. Her fingers contacted and curled around an ornate marble candlestick.

'Honey . . .' of a sudden he was too near, breathing all over her. 'I think a girl like you needs somebody. Why not me, baby? You're beautiful, baby . . .'

Simultaneously, as he made a grab for her, Amanda lifted the candlestick, but before she could do anything with it Veronica shrieked from the doorway behind them. Long afterwards that cry was to ring in Amanda's ears.

'You little slut!' Veronica screamed. 'Just what do you think you're doing? How dare you entice poor Herman!'

Entice poor Herman? Wide-eyed with shock, Amanda stared at her sister. She had certainly done no such thing! She knew it; Veronica knew it, but she hadn't waited to discover the truth. Yet, in that split second of stunned silence, as she stood speechless, Amanda realised it was the only way out. Veronica's first marriage had failed—this one must not! Quite clearly, perhaps because she knew her so well, Amanda read her sister's thoughts. For Veronica to put any other construction on the sordid little scene in front of her would spell doom to her hopes of future happiness; all her well-laid plans. And along with that happiness would go her outraged pride, Veronica's exaggerated sense of dignity, which must be preserved, come what might.

But it wasn't altogether this which caused Amanda to restrain the hot denial which rose impulsively to her lips. In the fraction of time while this went through her head she remembered Veronica's kindness, her generosity in helping her after their father had married again. In the space of seconds, it seemed, she could make or break Veronica's marriage and, whatever happened, she could never bear the responsibility of that. Of course there could be just a chance that Veronica might be willing to see reason. She said, rather desperately, 'It wasn't quite as you think, Veronica. You're jumping to all the wrong conclusions.' Meant to be pacifying, the words came out stiffly. Veronica was far from impressed.

'I suppose,' she said icily, 'that Herman thought the bathroom empty and came in by mistake.'

'Something like that . . .'

'Not really,' Herman, who had stood looking dumbfounded by his wife's unexpected appearance, now found his tongue and added clumsily to the nightmare. 'I heard Amanda shout. It seemed she was in some kind of trouble. I didn't stop to think, darling, I just charged in.'

And she had thought him slow-witted! Convulsively

9

Amanda swallowed a slither of pure hate, choking on a suddenly dry throat. Any further protest seemed futile. 'I think I'll go and pack a case,' she whispered, her face white. 'I guess I won't be going to America after all.'

'You certainly won't! Not with us, at any rate.' Veronica's furious reply hit Amanda sharply as she pushed past her out of the room, and Herman was left behind as Veronica followed her down the passage into her bedroom. In vain Amanda tried to stop her by closing the door.

Veronica burst it open, propelled, it seemed, by an unrestrained temper as she regarded Amanda's scantily clad figure. It was almost as if she was seeing her for the first time as a woman—grown and attractive, eclipsing the schoolgirl image which she had clung to for so long. 'I can see now,' she continued coldly, when Amanda didn't speak, 'that it was a mistake to ask you to come with us in the first place.'

At that Amanda turned, unable to stop herself retorting, 'You only asked me to go because you know no one in Washington and you were always terrified of being lonely. You begged me to go! You might recall that I wasn't too keen to go back again so soon. I only agreed because I didn't want to hurt you by refusing.'

Veronica ignored this, going curtly on as though Amanda hadn't spoken. 'You've changed! I hadn't realised how much. I should never have let you go with the Randalls. Obviously you've picked up habits you'd be better without.'

Amanda's head spun. 'The Randalls were your idea, too. You know that! They were your friends to begin with.'

Hurt beyond speech, Amanda turned from her sister's coldly accusing face. Suddenly, in a lightning flashback over the brief years of her life, she saw that the most formative periods had been almost wholly directed by Veronica. Boarding school had been Veronica's idea, although she hadn't gone to one herself. Then, after their father had married again, hadn't it been Veronica who had suggested that Amanda should live with her at the flat? And it had been two years later, when Amanda left school, that she had begged her to go to America with the Randalls, people whom she had got to know through her work, who had been rather desperate to find a reliable au pair girl to look after their two children, while the Randalls, both scientists, did research work in Florida.

'It will only be for six months,' she remembered Veronica saying. 'It will give you a breathing space. Time enough to decide what you really want to do. Bill Randall did me a good turn once, so I do owe him something. Besides, it's not very convenient for me to have you around right now. I may be busy.'

So without further protest Amanda had gone with the Randalls, but the six months had stretched into two years, during which they had been loath to part with her. Not until a letter had arrived from Veronica to say she had married again had Amanda suddenly realised she was twenty, and that life was somehow passing her by. With an urgent desire to return home came the knowledge that, very quickly, she must establish herself in some sort of career. That to remain in America, looking after children, wasn't exactly what she wanted. So she had left quickly, refusing to listen to the combined persuasions of the four Randalls, unwilling that they should make her change her mind.

Unfortunately she was to find her arrival in London marred by unforeseen problems. Because of Veronica's marriage she had anticipated staying with her father and stepmother on the small farm which Richard had inherited in Devon, but to her surprise Veronica had objected.

'You ought not to have come home, Amanda,' she had said. 'If you'd waited, instead of arriving out of the blue, you could have joined Herman and me in Washington. Herman has already promised to find you suitable employment, and you could also have helped me. Now we'll have the added expense of paying your fare back again.'

Amanda had only shrugged, not finding within herself the heart to argue, yet unable to completely understand Veronica's point of view. She had been married only three months.

Didn't she and Herman want to be on their own? Surely Herman could provide all the companionship Veronica needed, as well as alleviating the loneliness she seemed so desperately afraid of? Yet, to her surprise, Herman had added his pleas to Veronica's, and Amanda, against her better judgement, had given in.

It was really the only thing she could do, Veronica had told her firmly. It would have been little use going down to Devon. Eva, their stepmother, definitely wouldn't want her. Nor were the neighbours, with one or two exceptions, very friendly either. Daddy, of course, was always too busy, and Eva's word was law.

Amanda wasn't altogether gullible, but had decided it didn't really matter so very much. She had only spent two brief weekends on the farm herself, just before she had left school. It had rained heavily during both her visits, and her father had seemed preoccupied, not very interested in his young daughter. She couldn't remember much about Eva at all. She did remember, though, being secretly glad to return to London.

She had been determined, however, despite anything Veronica might say, to see the family before she went off again. But when she had announced her intentions, Veronica had explained that Richard, a well-known biologist, was in Central Nepal, somewhere near Sikkim, and that Eva was with him. They weren't expected home for another month. That had been almost three weeks ago, so it would be at least another week before they were back, Amanda calculated.

Now it seemed fairly obvious, family or no family, that she and Veronica had reached a parting of the ways, but before she went Amanda felt compelled to make one thing clear. Into the waiting silence she said quickly, 'The Randalls are nice! Work was perhaps the only bad habit they indulged in. We never had time for anything else.'

'You don't expect me to believe that!' Veronica raged. 'To think I trusted you! I arranged to meet Herman this

12

evening, as you know. What do you think I felt like when he didn't turn up?'

Hastily, feeling it futile to argue any further, Amanda snatched up an overnight bag, pushing into it a pair of pyjamas, a few other odds and ends before removing her bathrobe and scrambling into some clothes. While she dressed she was aware of Veronica watching with coldly critical eyes. 'You can send the rest of my things to Paddington,' she said.

'You're not going to Daddy!' Veronica's expression grew suddenly wary.

Jealousy again, Amanda decided, this time not really caring. If Veronica was so keen to be rid of her, could it matter where she went? She replied levelly, her voice devoid of emotion, 'As he's in Nepal that doesn't make sense. Wherever I go, I can collect my luggage more conveniently from Paddington. I might even go back to the Randalls,' she added, rather wildly.

'I doubt they'd have you!'

'Maybe not ...' Wearily, Amanda thrust bemused fingers across her forehead, glancing towards her large trunk, already packed and labelled for America. 'You'd better tear those labels off,' she said.

'With pleasure!' Clearly unforgiving, Veronica shut her mouth sharply. 'And I shouldn't advise you to go near the family, not even when they return. Certainly I shouldn't think they'd have you—not after they hear what I have to tell them!'

Two days later, as Amanda sat on the train to Devon, she could still see the wild, tormented anger on Veronica's face. It still seemed incredible that Veronica should have gone to such lengths about one small incident, that she had allowed her inborn jealousy to overrule common sense and lead her to believe the worst. She had still been throwing insults as Amanda left the flat. Herman had been nowhere to be seen. Amanda shivered in spite of the warmth of the train. Perhaps Veronica was not entirely to blame. The fault must surely lie with Herman, or perhaps it could be placed more

13

squarely on her own head for allowing herself to be persuaded to go to America with them in the first place!

Amanda had realised this as she had almost run from the flat. She had known then there could be no going back. That nothing anyone might say or do could retrieve the situation. There was only one sensible thing to do—absolutely imperative! She must keep out of Veronica's way. Even if Veronica had second thoughts and tried to contact her. For everyone's sake Amanda knew she must hide, and remain hidden until Veronica and Herman sailed.

Amanda stirred unhappily on her second-class seat. For all her well-meant resolutions, she was still fond of her sister, and it didn't help to know that Veronica was trying to get in touch with her, might indeed even now be looking for her. Amanda had learnt this when she had rung the elderly cousin who had been their housekeeper until Daddy had married again. Quite suddenly Amanda had known an urge to see her. She had also hoped to find a bed for a few nights. Staying in a hotel, she found, was a rather lonely business.

Unfortunately the cousin had a friend staying with her and couldn't accommodate Amanda. She didn't sound as though she even wanted to, and Amanda soon found out why. 'Veronica's been around,' the old woman shouted down the line. 'She's been looking for you everywhere. Said you'd run away. I don't want to be involved in any family quarrel!'

Quickly, with a mumbled word of thanks and farewell, Amanda had replaced the receiver, glancing furtively over her shoulder as she did so, half expecting Veronica to be lurking by her side. From that moment onwards she had panicked. If Veronica was looking for her, then there was every chance she would find her, especially if Herman was to give a hand. Working at the Embassy he might employ all kinds of tactics. And if Veronica wanted to find her it could only be to express a condescending forgiveness, to ask her to carry on with their plans as arranged. But Amanda knew quite clearly that she didn't want to go back to

14

America, and definitely not now, not after the fiasco with Herman!

Yet, if Veronica were to find her, how could she explain all this? Amanda's brow had knitted in very real perplexity. All her life, or for as long as she could remember, she had allowed herself to be dominated by her sister's stronger personality. Now, although not so willing to be overruled, Amanda was genuinely apprehensive of facing her, having little real doubt that after such a meeting she would find herself agreeing weakly to anything Veronica suggested.

With what seemed to be a brilliant flash of insight Amanda knew there was only one place where she might hope to avoid her. Devonshire! With the family away there was no one in the house. In the circumstances it was the last place where Veronica would think of looking. She could stay there on her own without anyone knowing, and in three or four days' time, with Veronica and Herman gone, she would be safe. And she could scarcely be accused of breaking the law by hiding in her parents' home. Without stopping to consider the wisdom of such a plan, Amanda had, with great haste, packed a rucksack, paid her hotel bill and rushed to buy a ticket to the West Country.

In the confined space of the compartment Amanda eased her long, slim legs as best she could and sighed. In retrospect this was all probably quite ridiculous, and it was silly to pretend she had a guilty conscience, especially when for the first time in her life she felt really free. Veronica was happily married and would be much better without her. Once in America she would soon settle down and make new friends. America was a very wonderful experience for anyone, married or single. Veronica would soon become absorbed in her new life and forget all about her young sister and one stupid little incident in a bathroom.

In a way, Amanda mused, lulled by the rhythm of iron wheels on an iron track, to stay at Combe Farm on her own was probably the best idea she had had for some time. It would certainly give her time to decide exactly what she was going to do. The salary which the Randalls had paid hadn't been very generous, although she had been treated as one of the family, but now she had very little left, just enough to see her through until she found another job, which shouldn't take long.

The train ran through Exeter and she left it at Newton Abbot to catch a bus. Unfortunately, after this, she made her first mistake by getting out at the wrong village and had to wait an hour for another bus!

'It's easily done,' the driver commented, when she ruefully related what had happened. 'You're a stranger in these parts, then, miss?'

'Sort of . . .' she mumbled, aware of the man's curious stare, annoyed at having drawn attention to herself in this manner when it was essential she remained anonymous.

But much the same thing occurred when at last she arrived at Ashburton and went in search of a taxi. Because of the time she had so foolishly lost, the November afternoon was rapidly darkening, and, to her dismay, Amanda found she could remember few landmarks in the bleak countryside. A taxi would appear to be essential. Deliberately she had timed her arrival, hoping that in the dusk of late afternoon no one would notice her, but she had forgotten just how dark a country area could be. Such secrecy, she realised, might be silly, yet she knew that in small communities, especially during winter, a stranger was quickly noticed. Should Veronica, pursuing every possibility, ring up a friend in the neighbourhood, then she might easily learn of Amanda's presence and come to the right conclusions. Determined to eliminate even the slightest risk, Amanda resolved to take every precaution!

Surely it must be the easiest thing in the world to slip into a taxi without undue comment? Amanda had done it dozens of times. This taxi driver, however, seemed to regard her bedraggled appearance, her lack of luggage with suspicion. So much suspicion, it seemed, that he asked her twice about it, obviously not satisfied with her evasive reply. But how could she explain to the man, if indeed it was any of his business, that she hadn't any luggage because her

16

sister hadn't sent it to Paddington, or anywhere else, so far as she could discover? It seemed clear that Veronica was hanging on to it until the last moment, and it was this fact above all others that convinced Amanda that Veronica was continuing with her search.

'I just want to go a few miles down the road,' she muttered, as she climbed in beside him, hoping vaguely he wouldn't probe any further. Despite the dampness of her apparel she was startled that the man evidently mistook her for a boy, addressing her as 'young fellow', a mistake which Amanda, on second thoughts, decided not to rectify. As a boy she might be safer from suspicion.

'I can't think where you can be off to on a night like this!' the man retorted gruffly, casting a sideways glance over a shivering Amanda. 'Do you know what time it is?'

'It's only five o'clock,' Amanda protested with some bewilderment, keeping her voice low..

'Five o'clock,' the man snorted, 'on a November night on Dartmoor. Rain and snow coming down! Just proves how much sense you've got. Beats me why a young fellow like yourself wouldn't choose to stay at home. You look as though a whiff of wind would blow you away.'

Amanda shrugged, with more bravado than she actually felt. The man was probably right, although she would have died rather than admit it. The weather was really vile and she felt chilled to the bone, and longed suddenly for a hot bath and a meal, in that order. In her rucksack she had food, enough to last for several days, and, once in the house, she would soon have a fire going. She refused to dwell on the possibility that the place might be barred up too thoroughly for her to get in. She could scarcely ask this man to wait— or to assist her in breaking and entering!

Through the driving wind and snow she thought she saw a sign which said Combe Farm. She couldn't be sure, but when she asked the driver he nodded and she immediately asked to be put down. 'I'll walk the few yards back,' she told him, pressing the fare into his hand. 'I might even go on a bit further.' Her deliberate attempt to mislead him was to be her undoing, only she didn't realise it until afterwards.

Once out on the cold dark road her wavering confidence deserted as the craziness of her plan suddenly hit her. The taxi waited obligingly until she found her torch, then roared off with a derisive farewell hoot into the night, leaving her standing, a solitary figure, enveloped in a shroud of swirling snow.

Momentarily Amanda remained where she was until her eyes grew accustomed to the grey light. Her father had inherited this small estate shortly after he had remarried and, without hesitation, had sold his London home and moved in. This had been almost five years ago. Now, with a peculiar ache in her heart, Amanda wished things had been different, that she had gone with them. One could scarcely blame Eva for not taking much interest in a stepdaughter who had shown no great desire to know her. Amanda shrugged, as she started off. Might not it all be wishful thinking? Veronica had spent a lot of time here while Amanda had been in America, and she had remarked on several occasions that Eva hadn't put herself out to be kind. Amanda's own two weekends she could barely remember, and she didn't suppose there was much point in thinking about them now as she trudged along.

The brunt of the storm didn't seem to hit her until she turned the first bend. There she caught the full force of sleet and wind, a full concentration of the elements which battered and spun her until she stumbled and fell hard into an overgrown ditch. Feeling decidedly the worse for wear, she pulled herself out, laughing almost hysterically at her plight, aware of soft tears mingling with the rain on her cheeks. Quickly she sobered up, suddenly frightened. If she didn't pull herself together, she might still be lying here come morning. People still perished in storms, and she still had some way to go. With determination she forced her tired legs to continue, running and slithering along the last few yards of lane. Until, with a final spurt, she reached the house. Relief, swift and palpitating, washed over her, and she moved, a sudden rush, her hair beneath her woollen cap haloed with snow, blue denim jacket plastered about her, wet through, yet staring at the house, a black shape, scarcely discernible, looming through the darkness in front of her.

Coming to a sudden halt, she swept a slightly shaking hand across her face, brushing the snow from her lashes, and with it a long strand of wet hair from her eyes. Her fingers caught the edge of her cap, lifting it slightly, and the rising wind did the rest, whipping it from her head, blowing it away. Oh, well, what did it matter? She was home now. Why bother about the loss of one small hat?

All the same, the rain through her hair was uncomfortable, even though the rest of her was soaked. Taking a few tentative steps forwards, she flashed her torch around, surveying the old stone façade of the house. The sooner she was inside the better. She was probably no less susceptible to pneumonia than anyone else.

It was quite obvious that the place was deserted. Although Amanda had known what to expect, she could not suppress a faint shudder of dismay as her glance fell on the unlit windows. A light in just one of them, she thought wistfully, would have been a most welcome sight. It soon became equally obvious that the doors were all locked securely. Stumbling against one, she gave a gigantic push, but it didn't budge an inch. It was then that she recalled vaguely an attic window which had always been open. Just slightly open, but Eva had complained that the rain came in and ran through to the bedroom below, and no one, she had said, would see about getting it repaired!

Daddy had never repaired anything in his life! It had been a family joke, and Amanda prayed—actually prayed—he hadn't changed. There might be a chance, if only slight, that the window would still be the same.

Several minutes later, having negotiated the back of the house and found a ladder, Amanda stared almost happily up at the window, relieved to find it was much as it used to be. In the wavering light from her torch she noted the slight gap between the top of the window and the frame which no one might have noticed if they hadn't known what to look for.

19

'Thank goodness for that,' said Amanda aloud.

The window, set in the sloping attic roof, wasn't so high, but without the ladder it would have been impossible to climb up. It had been, she silently acknowledged, a slice of sheer luck to have found one so handy, and rather fervently she hoped her luck would hold. The roof looked slippery, half covered as it was with snow, but if she was careful it should present no insurmountable problem.

The ladder was very like the one which she had used often when working for the Randalls. The twins had been over-fond of climbing trees! Gently she eased out the extension, working as quickly as she could with frozen fingers, then propped it against the wall. It appeared secure when she tested it. With only a dim light it was difficult to be sure. She must just try it and see.

Lifting her rucksack firmly on to her back, she crawled up the rungs, her body shivering in its thin covering. Desperately she was beginning to realise she had to get in—her head felt most peculiar. If she couldn't reach the attic window, then she must break in down below. Perhaps she had been foolish not to do so in the first place.

Concentrating completely on the task in front of her, Amanda never heard the footsteps beneath her. Perhaps, on the blanket of freshly fallen snow, the man's light approach had been silent, any sound impossible to hear above the wild howl of the wind. Whatever it was, she was totally unprepared for the threatening shout which rang thunderously in her ears. A voice, which seemed to hold more force than the storm itself, demanding to know what she was up to.

Afterwards, a long time afterwards, Amanda was to regard the phrasing of that question with some amusement, but her views, in retrospect, were far divorced from her terror in that panic-stricken moment. A moment when her heart jerked in her breast with a frightening intensity, and her numbed hands lost their grip on the thin wooden slats. In the split second, as she turned, in a blind panic, her glance fell on the man below. Illuminated in the light from the storm lantern he held, he appeared huge, menacing, a pagan image straight from some heathen corner of Dartmoor. It was there in his face, curiously etched against the darkness, brutally at one with the elements.

'Come down off that ladder,' he repeated, 'or I'll tip you straight off into the snow!'

That cool, controlled voice had a ludicrous effect. She stiffened into rigidity, her hands slipping as she lost her balance. Then she was falling, her feet slithering from the ladder, and her voice, released suddenly from the frozen regions of her throat, came with a wild cry of despair. There was only a fraction of time, just one flash of awareness before she fell, enveloped in his answering shout of impatience. Then her head hit the corner of a jutting piece of roof and there came merciful oblivion. She knew nothing of the strong arms which enfolded her as her unconscious body tumbled the last few feet to the ground.

She came to a little while later, conscious of pain, of someone forcing brandy between her cold lips. The same person was holding her firmly, in some enclosed space, sheltered from the storm. This was only a fleeting impression as she lifted weighted eyelids, as she attempted to see clearly the face floating above her own. It seemed there might be a thread of relief in the voice that spoke to her.

'When I told you to come down off that ladder, I didn't mean you to take me so literally, young man! We don't take too kindly to intruders in this part of the world, but we don't wish them any particular harm. The police will deal with you.'

Helplessly Amanda knew she must have dreamt that thread of relief. Indignant anger surged in spite of the awful pain at the side of her head. It registered vaguely that, like the taxi driver, he thought she was a boy, but not even this seemed to justify his brutal comment. His face still swam hazily, and it could have been the brandy which gave her the strength to retort sharply, 'I could have been killed. You choose not to think of that!'

She might have known he would have the diabolical nerve to grin maliciously, 'But you weren't, were you? Perhaps you deserve to be worse than you are. Young vagabonds who roam the countryside should learn not to complain if fate doesn't always deal with them kindly. You break into property, then expect the owner to take a lenient view. If I had my way, youths like you would all be under lock and key.'

Over Amanda was sweeping a peculiar nausea which she strove to control. Her teeth were chattering, the pain in her head unbearable, yet from somewhere she gathered enough courage to reply, 'It's men like you who ought to be shut up!' Her remark might be quite unreasonable, she knew, but somehow, if such a thing were possible, it made her feel better.

She didn't allow for the manner in which his arms fell away with a punishing abruptness, and without support she slumped back, unable to save herself. Faintly, above a strange roaring in her ears, she heard his muttered expletive as he grabbed her roughly again. This time he propped her up harshly on the seat of the Land Rover, securing a seat belt tightly around her, pushing her head none too gently to the side of the door as nausea overtook her. In a few moments it was over, then once more Amanda knew nothing as she slid luxuriously into a sea of soft, wavering darkness.

# CHAPTER TWO

Amanda's head ached. On second thoughts it didn't actually ache, it pounded, and her whole body seemed to be throbbing with heat. Suddenly frightened, she lay quite still, not knowing where she was, suspended in space like some lost spirit crying out for recognition. Where was she—what was she doing here? She was only aware that she lay on something soft. This much was slowly becoming apparent.

She took a deep breath and it hurt, so carefully she tried to open her eyes. There was a light above her head. It swirled, filling her whole vision, almost blinding her. It was a pitiless, dancing light, creating bizarre images, demi-gods who rose up and shrieked at her. They were potentially dangerous, so quietly, so they wouldn't notice, she let her heavy lashes fall, concentrating wholly with her mind.

Feeling totally inadequate she tried to marshal her wayward illusions into some semblance of order. With nervous hands, as if she were playing a game, she attempted to explore her immediate vicinity. It might be she was hurt in some way and was lying on a bed. Surely nothing else could be so comfortable, and there were pillows, she thought, beneath her head. Cautiously, like some small child afraid of the unknown, she turned on to her side hoping that the movement, any movement, would jerk some hidden chord of her memory. As if to assist it she forced her reluctant thoughts backwards until, with another flash of blinding light, it came, so easily, so devastatingly, like an avalanche, bringing with it shock and total consternation.

With the gasp which escaped her taut lips, Amanda's fingers went swiftly to her temples, attempting to block out the picture of her own folly—to soften the blow.

How could she have been so foolish? For one brief second she prayed this might be a nightmare from which she would wake up. The farm, the house, the window and the ladder all came back to taunt her, parading with the cruel demons who already mocked her. Then as her demons paraded, there came the shape of one who had shouted. The human one, who had caused her to fall and hurt her head. A man with a face as dark as the night about him!

'Oh, no . . .' she moaned aloud, as full realization followed quickly, flooding her memory with every tiny detail. How could he have known she was there? Perhaps she was already in the hands of the police, about to be accused of breaking and entering—something which she'd joked about previously. Or worse still, whoever it was who had waylaid her had probably already contacted the flat. Veronica could be on her way! 'Oh, no,' Amanda repeated again, despairingly.

With renewed alarm she forced her eyes open, this time to focus clearly on her immediate surroundings. The room was large, obviously a bedroom, and comfortably though plainly furnished. But not Combe Farm, of that she was certain. She couldn't recall any apartment such as this. The bed was king-size, huge and canopied, she herself a small ridge in the middle of it. The carpet seemed deep with a smooth pile, and across the windows the curtains hung in wide folds of fine, soft velvet, effectively muting the sounds of the storm outside.

Nervously Amanda stirred, dragging her eyes away from the window. The central heating must be turned up because she was hot—too hot. Unless it was the thought of Veronica which caused the heat to pour through her aching body. Surely a blow on the head couldn't be sufficient to make her feel like this? Rather desperately she pushed back against her pillows, struggling to sit upright. Where was everybody? Oughtn't there to be someone here? It seemed she had been abandoned, left to die, while whoever it was who had brought her here regaled himself in another part of the house.

Her eyes wide, the pupils dilated like a young gazelle ready for flight, Amanda tensed, waiting, but there was only silence, apart from the fiendish scream of the wind. Then gradually a vibration impinged upon her ears, growing louder and louder. Somewhere in the house a telephone was ringing, the stringent tones echoing shrilly, until suddenly it stopped. Someone had apparently picked up the receiver, although she could hear no sound of a voice.

Swiftly, making up her mind in one impulsive moment, she flung back the sheets which covered her and rolled out of bed, fighting the wave of faintness which caught her as she swung her feet to the ground. Steadying herself, she stared with some bewilderment at the clothes she was wearing. She was dressed in what appeared to be a man's pyjama jacket. Smooth, like silk, a beautiful fine material, which clung to her slender figure, reaching almost to her knees. Below it her long, slim legs were bare, the skin flawless, still faintly tanned from her stay in America. Apart from this one thin garment she didn't have another stitch on. Whoever had undressed her had done a thorough job!

Regaining her balance after a few seconds, although still feeling decidedly peculiar, Amanda made her way towards the door. No good could come of contemplating that which could not be helped. Obviously she must have been wet through, and after all, it had been her own silly fault. It was essential now that she found the lady of the house, to thank her as quickly as possible before arranging to be on her way. No doubt the people here would be glad to see the last of her.

After letting herself silently out on to the narrow corridor she stood very still, her well-shaped head on one side, listening. Somewhere down in the lower regions someone was talking. The sound was faint, but she could definitely hear it. Stealthily, on bare feet, Amanda crept along the passage, a little nearer to the top of the stairs. Here the stout oaken balustrade allowed her to look down into the hall below.

As she had suspected, someone was using the telephone. As she craned forward, her forehead pressed against the wooden slats, an almost audible exclamation escaped her. She could see the man who was speaking, not very clearly as he had his back towards her, but she had little doubt, from the extreme darkness of his head, the forcefulness of his voice, that it was the same man who had been the cause of all her misfortunes. The same man who'd tipped her off the ladder, perhaps inadvertently, but he had been responsible all the same. It was he, she felt sure, who had literally dosed her with brandy and held her with such indifferent detachment when she had been sick.

For a moment, too stunned to move, Amanda stared, clutching the rails tightly with agitated fingers. This house, wherever it was, must belong to him. If nothing else his careless demeanour against the telephone proclaimed it. Of course she might have guessed he would bring her here, considering the way he'd almost thrown her into his Land Rover, but her mind was still confused, the events of the last few hours coming back only slowly. Then suddenly, as she leant nearer pondering with some bewilderment on a suitable course of action, she heard him saying quite clearly to the person he was talking to.

'You have no reason to worry, Veronica. I can assure you that everything is as it should be. I had a card from Richard only this morning. He doesn't expect to be home for another week, so it would be pointless to come down, especially when you're so busy arranging to get away. If it's any consolation there's a storm raging and I should think we might be cut off for several days. You know what storms can be like on Dartmoor.'

Veronica? In the slight pause which followed, as he listened while his caller answered, Amanda remained tense with apprehension. It must be her sister! The bit about Richard, who was their father, confirmed it. It would be a remarkable coincidence if this was not so. Intently she concentrated, every nerve tight. The man was speaking again, his voice even from this distance seemingly lighter.

'I quite agree, Veronica, you can't let Herman down. You must go to America. Herman certainly won't want to go alone. And if you sail in four days' time Richard wouldn't expect you to make a special trip in weather like this just to see that the farm's okay, although I'll tell him you rang.'

26

Another pause, then his voice again, softly ironical yet with undertones of laughter. 'A bride of three months ought not to say such things, my dear. If circumstances had been different, who knows.' His wide shoulders lifted, indicating a faintly rueful smile at the corners of his mouth. 'As it is,' he continued, 'I'll look forward to seeing you when you come back.'

How dared he! Blind anger did nothing to disperse Amanda's general feeling of delirium. The whole situation seemed even more incongruous than it had a few minutes ago. How dared he make love to Veronica, because that, as clear as daylight, was what he'd been up to! Amanda might reluctantly confess to being without a deal of experience, but she was no fool. The tender, anticipatory note in his voice spoke for itself. Every syllable had held a caress—were all men tarred with the same brush! First Herman—now him! Furiously from her lofty perch, Amanda flung down total condemnation, in that instance completely disillusioned with every man she could think of.

Not until a long time afterwards did she stop to consider Veronica's part in that little intrigue. As the murmur of the man's deep voice continued, Amanda's only concern after her first wrath was that Veronica should not discover she was here. For four days, until Veronica and Herman sailed, she must contrive to preserve some anonymity whatever the cost. Perhaps in a way it had been decreed by a protective God that she should overhear this telephone conversation. Otherwise she might never have known of the friendship between Veronica and the man below, and to be forewarned was to be forearmed, or so it was said!

Swiftly, feeling fractionally better, Amanda turned, intent on preserving what secrecy she could. Then suddenly, to her utter chagrin, she sneezed—not a delicate, orientated kind of sneeze which might have passed unnoticed, but a loudly undignified paroxysm of sound, guaranteed to attract attention. The gods, it would seem, had deserted her!

To Amanda, crouching palpitating amongst the shadows, the dropping of the telephone receiver was an explosion in her ears. The relegating sound of plastic hitting plastic as the man swung abruptly, his eyes, across the dividing space, pinning hers, his glance the calculating glance of a stranger. Unable to stir, her heartbeats magnified by her heightening awareness, she was struck immobile by the weight of a peculiar tension. Even from here she could see that his was a hard, handsome face, the face of a man totally self-reliant, with the ability to hit always harder than his opponent. Tall, dark, broad-shouldered, lean-hipped, virile ... Amanda thought she might go on for ever. He was also, she told herself severely, for fear some part of her got the wrong impression, a philanderer. Not a trait to be admired under any circumstances!

Only this much had she time to digest as, without removing his eyes from her face, he was up the stairs in a trice, one hand beneath her elbow, sweeping her ruthlessly to her feet, steadying her grimly when she lost her balance. She flushed and foolishly resented getting caught again.

'If you're not back to bed within seconds,' he said, 'you'll wish to goodness that I'd left you to perish in the snow!' He took no notice of her flushed cheeks, her faintly indignant air, as he thrust her before him sharply down the passage, like a bundle of rags he could dispose of at any minute should he so wish.

Once in the large bedroom, Amanda tried to shake off his hand. The whole of her body was throbbing with heat and a sickly kind of excitement. It seemed a ridiculous moment to tell herself she'd never cared for a man with green eyes. Beautiful eyes, clear and luminous though his might be, they held all the coolness of a rock pool and were just about as intimidating. She turned a vivid face to him, determined he shouldn't guess how ill she was feeling.

'I don't want to go back to bed, and you can't make me! I must be on my way. If I might have my clothes, then perhaps I can thank your wife for her assistance. I'd be very much obliged if you would also ring for a taxi.'

'I don't have any wife.' He watched her narrowly, his tone mild enough, even slightly bored. He ignored her request for clothing and a taxi. He didn't even ask if she felt strong enough to travel. Obviously her state of health was a matter of sheer indifference to him.

Heavily Amanda floundered, her thoughts going around in circles. 'No wife?' she repeated, stupidly, with an almost vague bewilderment. Somehow she had known a man like this would be married. He must be well into his thirties and the type that would appeal to most women, and his was surely a face of some experience, of diabolical self-assurance. It seemed she had jumped to the wrong conclusions. She remembered his conversation with Veronica. Apparently he indulged in affairs with other men's wives, thus relegating the necessity of having one of his own. Tentatively she tried again. 'Your mother, then, or whoever it is who runs the house for you?'

'No mother, either. I live on my own.' The green eyes seemed to dance ironically, or it might have been a trick of the light. 'I'm sure such a circumstance shouldn't worry an independent young lady like you.'

Stunned, Amanda sank down on to the bed against which she had been defiantly standing. She closed her eyes, attempting to shut out his derisive face as shock raced through her. She was creamy pale, her forehead faintly beaded with perspiration. If there was no woman in the house, then who had undressed her? She certainly hadn't been wearing a pyjama top when she'd arrived at Combe Farm! Surely this man couldn't have—wouldn't have . . . ? Why, she didn't even know his name. Nor did she particularly want to. She couldn't even bear to think that he had touched her. She had been unconscious—there lay the only grain of comfort. Making a superhuman effort, she opened her eyes wide and looked straight at him. Quite clearly, from the expression in his, he had read her thoughts. 'You appear to find it amusing, Mr . . . er . . . whoever you are!' She thought her tone of voice devastating.

He gave a short laugh, the glint in his eye deepening. 'If you'd chosen to mention that you were a girl it would have made little difference. You were wet through, scarcely the time for false modesty. Even now I should think you're running quite a high temperature, and yet you talk of being on your way! Why, you haven't even got a penny in your pocket!'

Alarm jerked Amanda up to her feet again as a tremor shot through her—a surge of dismay, quickly to be replaced by sheer fright. In her handbag she had had quite a sum of money, more, probably, than it had been wise to carry, and certainly enough to meet any contingency. More than enough to take her to the nearest hotel, where she should have had the sense to go in the first place! Yet this man said he hadn't found a penny. 'My bag?' she gasped, her eyes dilated pools of blank dismay.

'If you mean your rucksack,' he muttered dryly, 'which was all you had with you, I went through that very thoroughly. I presumed to find some form of identity—a telephone number, perhaps. Somewhere where I might have contacted anxious parents. But all you appeared to possess was a meagre supply of basic rations. Like most of your kind you obviously choose to travel light.'

His mouth compressed as his eyes travelled over her, filled with censure, yet with a hint of something else. Amanda, however, didn't notice, nor for a second did she speak; his unflattering remarks went over her head. Desperately anxious about her handbag, she couldn't think where it might have gone. Only vaguely did she seem to recall leaving the taxi. The lane to the farm was only a snow-filled memory, too hazy to reconstruct. No matter how she applied herself she couldn't remember losing her handbag, and to have lost it she must! Instinctively she knew that this man, who had chosen not to give his name when she had almost pointedly asked, was not a thief. He might have taken her pride when he had removed her clothing, but anything he chose to steal would have no relative value. She must take into account, of course, that he was totally ruthless—it was there in the set of his head, the brilliance of his gaze, the taut line of his well-shaped, sensuous mouth. Whatever happened, she vowed as she had vowed before, he mustn't discover her identity. The loss of her bag would be minimal compared with the disastrous repercussions of this! To be hauled back to town by Veronica, who could be strangely persuasive when it came to getting her own way, was more than Amanda dared think about. Anything—almost anything— was preferable to that.

Hopefully, controlling an inner agitation, she glanced at her inquisitor, intent on evasion while retaining a modicum of truth. 'I have no anxious parents,' she murmured carefully. 'I did have a very little money, but it seems I must have dropped it somewhere. Perhaps I could borrow a few pounds? Just enough to see me through. I should only be a nuisance if I stayed here.'

His brilliant glance met hers, staying on her transparent young face. 'You're already that,' he mocked bluntly. 'You and your kind are a nuisance to the community. I shouldn't wish to be personally responsible for inflicting you upon them. Country people have enough to do in weather like this without adding to their burdens. Besides, if I were to lend you money, what chance would I have of ever seeing it again?'

'You can't keep me here against my will!' Stung by his detestable attack, Amanda retaliated wildly, aroused beyond the limits of discretion, wanting to hurt him as he hurt her, even while realizing the futility of such an endeavour. He might have been kinder; he could have shown one twinge of compassion; it might have occurred to him that there could be extenuating circumstances. But no, his glance was wholly derisive, the glance of a man who had no time, or patience, with human frailty. Perhaps, Amanda admitted, he was justified in some of his opinions, but he hadn't given her the benefit of one single doubt. She might have been anyone lost or in distress, she didn't necessarily have to be a rootless delinquent, a vagabond roaming the face of the earth. Well, let him think what he liked! No longer did she feel in any way indebted to him. His unsparing condemnation had at least absolved her from that. 'I'm sorry I asked you for anything,' she added stiffly, resenting his watching cynicism. 'Neither should I wish to worry your neighbours. If I could just have my clothes?'

'You're too ill.' It was a statement, not to be questioned. His voice was smooth, on an even keel, containing, surprisingly, a thread of patience, almost as if something about the situation intrigued him in spite of himself. Almost as if he was prepared to humour her fractionally.

Yet she persisted. 'If you think I'm ill, why don't you ring your local doctor? I'm sure you exaggerate, but he could set your mind at rest.' She didn't add that a doctor might also provide a means of escape. If she appealed to him he might be persuaded to take her back to town.

'I was coming to that,' his mouth shaped laconically. 'I've been trying to get hold of a doctor all evening—for advice only, I might say—but all the roads are blocked with snow, he could never get here in person. Maybe you don't know about Dartmoor in a blizzard, but we locals have learnt to treat such weather with respect.'

With a sinking heart Amanda stared at him, not doubting the authenticity of what he said. Mutely she shook her head. There would seem to be no escape. Yet he couldn't expect her to give in gracefully, although did she have any other alternative. Not wishing to consider the complications of this point, she confessed fretfully, 'I don't know anything about Dartmoor, in a storm or otherwise.'

'Then when were you here?' he shot at her, his derisive tone having little regard for the precarious state of her health.

'Here—oh . . .' she glanced at him blankly a full minute before she understood. Quickly she looked away from him, something—surely not her wits, saving her. 'I think it was during the summer, years ago.'

'Years ago?' His voice was sharp with a kind of wary impatience. 'You've certainly been to Combe Farm before, otherwise you wouldn't have known about that window. You couldn't have spotted it otherwise as it was almost covered with snow, and the chap with the taxi told me himself that it was already dark when he left you.'

So that was how he had found out! He had some sort of liaison with that crabby old taxi-driver! Bitterly she reflected he would never miss a thing. A master-mind for detail! The odd thing was he hadn't asked her name. A girl's only defence against a man like this would be to play it cool. He couldn't very well shake the information out of her. Dumbly she said, 'All large houses have attic windows, usually with some defect. I was only guessing, and I happened to be lucky—or so I thought until you came along.'

'You could have been luckier,' he agreed blandly, his darkening expression indicating that he did not for one moment believe her sorry little tale. 'You could have managed to creep inside, only to find a cold tomb of a house in which you might easily have perished.'

'I could have switched on the electricity. I should soon have warmed up.' Her widening eyes flew to his face, unconscious how illogical her argument.

'Wrong again, Miss Persistence,' his green eyes were as malicious as a cats. 'The current is off, and the cupboard containing the switches padlocked. Next time, before you break into a building, you should check.'

And he enjoyed even the mental spectacle of her freezing to death! He had the nerve to suggest she should be grateful, yet even his care hadn't prevented her from catching a terrible cold. Quickly she turned her head as she sneezed violently again. At that moment she could imagine no nicer fate than to be allowed to lie down quietly and die. 'Next time,' she murmured bitterly, 'I'll do just that.' She wasn't exactly sure to what she was alluding.

'That's better.' A look of deliberation seemed to harden his face. 'Who knows what other surprises you might have in store for you.'

'You could be right!' How could she tell him she wanted no more surprises? Since she had arrived home from America life had been full of them, and none of them pleasant. For the life of her Amanda couldn't think how one thing could evolve so easily, yet mistakenly, from another. But the fact remained, she had been caught up in a series of silly events from which her own stupidity had in no way extricated her. Confused, she blinked into the dark, enigmatic face so near her own. 'Nothing,' she tacked on vaguely, 'ever seems to turn out as one expects.'

'Not when you're leading this sort of life!'

'Why, you sound just like my father!' Suddenly, unaccountably she giggled, unaware of his sharpening glance. Softly, as her slightly hysterical laughter subsided, the urge to argue further deserted her, and she stared at him again with some of her former bewilderment, all eyes, very large and expressive, as tormented as a turbulent summer sea. Familiar tremors were once more evading her limbs, and everything receded in the most peculiar fashion. Again the room started playing tricks, the ceiling wavering ridiculously, the floor coming up to meet her, and not to be outdone, the storm outside roaring with a most frightening loudness in her ears. It seemed all too much, combined with the impregnable strength of the man before her. She felt as weak as a kitten, and just as helpless under his dissecting green eyes. With the faintest of frowns etching her smooth brow, Amanda subsided back on to her bed and promptly passed out.

When she woke it was morning; she knew it was morning because of the change of light. It slanted from a different angle, not directly above her head any more, and the quality was different, a cold, transparent grey, not interesting enough to invite further contemplation, so she prepared to go back to sleep. When someone spoke she knew a small, unreasonable surge of resentment.

'You're making too great a habit of this, young lady. I warn you, if you pass out on me again I won't be responsible for my reactions.'

The voice plummeted, discordant on her ears; smooth, of even timbre, nothing in the tone to disturb the superb aura of drowsy comfort which cocooned her like cottonwool. It was only the precise context of the words which she found irritating.

Slowly, from a vague feeling that it was expected of her, she opened her eyes, her wavering glance at first refusing to focus. Dark patches trembled until, through the mistiness, a man's face shaped from the shadows. That man! Shock caused her to blink, clearing miraculously last remnants of fog. This time the confusion disappeared completely, along with the cotton-wool!

'Who are you?' she whispered, staring up at him, her pale fingers suddenly clutching his arm as if trying to convey that the question was important to her. Beneath the thin material of his shirt she could feel the hard muscles flexing, and a tremor shot through her. She couldn't remember whether he was friend or foe. He didn't appear to be either.

His green eyes regarded her with a great detachment, but he obliged, if a little ironically. 'Jason Meade, at your service, ma'am. And yours?'

She couldn't mistake his meaning, but her own name curiously evaded her. A closed door refused to open in her mind. With a soft bewilderment she brushed taut fingers across her forehead. 'I can't remember,' she told him.

At once he withdrew, tilting backwards in his chair so that her hand slid from his arm. Yet there lurked in his face a hint of impatient concern. 'If I could believe that—' he frowned, his eyes intent on her face. 'You gave yourself an almighty thump on your head. Can't you really recall a thing?'

'Of course ...' Amanda felt the nerves of her stomach tightening. She could remember so much! 'It's just my name!'

'You could mean you don't want to tell me? For your information, I've nursed you through a day and a couple of nights. You could perhaps owe me that little bit of advice!'

Her widening eyes stayed on his face, the colour intensifying as, startled, she attempted to concentrate. A day and two nights. If nothing else it meant Veronica hadn't yet

35

sailed! Slowly, as she digested this, something else clicked into place. She was Amanda Trent who must remain in hiding until her sister left for America. Indelibly on her sub-consciousness must be impressed the need for continued silence—nothing else could have stopped her from giving herself away! This man employed devious methods. He had probed for information, knowing she was in no fit state to withhold it. Only her guardian angel could have saved her. He also supplied a fictitious name!

'I'm sorry,' she whispered, hastily squashing an uncomfortable twinge of guilt which plagued her in spite of her neat calculations. 'You're quite right, I do owe you something, and it's all coming back. I'm Miranda Smith.' In London, once, they had had a charlady called Miranda Smith. There must be thousands of Miranda Smiths! This one had been particularly obliging, and Amanda was sure she wouldn't object to anyone borrowing her name. Wrapped in a warm blanket of smugness, Amanda smiled sweetly up at Jason Meade. 'You can call me Miss Smith,' she said ingenuously.

His mouth firmed, still with a trace of irony. 'If you don't mind I'll try Miranda. After the informality of the last two days anything else might strain the credibility. A name isn't all that important, but it's convenient.'

'I suppose so.' Her voice was husky, the necessity to break away from that unwavering scrutiny uppermost in her mind. Obviously he didn't quite believe her, but was prepared to let it slide. In spite of a peculiar lethargy she felt her cheeks stain rose-red as the other side of his remark hit her forcibly. She guessed, from the way he said it, that, since he had brought her here, there had been no one else around. They had been alone together! In country districts, she supposed, this would be commonly known as flouting the conventions. Not many would take into account that she had been ill for most of the time. And she must surely have been ill, otherwise she couldn't possibly feel so weak. She braced herself, pushed back her hair and drew a deep breath.

'You said,' she began carefully, 'that I've been here quite a while. Have I been very ill?'

'You could say that . . .' His chin lifted, dropping again slightly. 'At a guess I should say you've just missed pneumonia. Risking another guess, I should say you're in fairly good condition, otherwise you couldn't have fought it off.'

If he were a farmer he could be talking of some of his own livestock! For a fleeting moment her eyes slipped to his chin. His chin was decided, even aggressive. His mouth mobile and sensuous, as she had thought before. His shoulders were dauntingly broad. Not a man to be argued with or taken lightly—or to be deceived in any way. Something inside her filled with odd little tremblings and she said quickly, 'I can't remember being really ill. I believe I did catch all the usual childish things, measles and such like, but nothing since.'

'Possibly because of the outdoor life you lead,' he noted disparagingly. 'It's a mistake, however, to think you're permanently immune. Things usually catch up on one sooner or later—even the most hardened criminals will tell you that.'

'I thought we were talking about illness,' she retorted sharply, not liking the way his continued allusions to her questionable status were beginning to hurt. Colour swept into her face, then just as suddenly left it again as she slumped back against her pillows, strangely and utterly spent. Fencing with him, coping with even the simplest twisting of words, was proving an intolerable strain.

She didn't notice that his glance went over her keenly, assessing the paleness of her cheeks, the dark shadows hollowed beneath her eyes, her general air of exhaustion. But she did notice when he rose to his feet and walked towards the door. Dismay surged through her heart in a confusing fashion as she watched him leaving, a frightening feeling of desolation she couldn't account for. Was he still annoyed with her? Perhaps she had spoken too impulsively. 'Where are you going?' she asked nervously.

'I'm going to make you a drink,' he announced coolly. 'It

will give you a chance to settle down, otherwise you'll be talking yourself into a relapse. I ought to have thought of it sooner. You're too diverting, Miranda, with your sharp little tongue.'

Ignoring the last bit of his discourse, she protested feebly, 'I'm not particularly thirsty. You might only be wasting your time.'

'Not my time, Miranda.' He turned to grin over his shoulder dryly as he disappeared through the door. 'There happens to be a lady who's giving me a hand. She's been singularly obliging so I don't want her upset. I should advise you to swallow whatever she chooses to bring without protest. She's known to be a bit of a tyrant—so be warned!'

Amanda stared in his direction long after he'd gone. So there had been someone else in the house after all! Indignation blended strangely with a touch of relief. He might have told her! Not, she assured herself hastily, that she had been worrying, but at least it was nice to know that the priorities had been observed. It might make things slightly easier in the problem-strewn future which she didn't want to think about.

Jason Meade ... Slowly she whispered his name aloud, feeling ridiculously daring. What sort of a man was he? she wondered. He was certainly an attractive one with his dark good looks. The sort of man for which any woman might spare a second glance. It was his expression which Amanda didn't like. His face, even in repose, was too hard and brooding. Almost as if he had sampled all life had to offer, and was disillusioned. Yet, just before he had left, she had been beginning to imagine him more approachable. Perhaps she was wrong? Perhaps there was nothing in that dark countenance to encourage anyone, let alone a mere girl!

Impatient with herself and the trend of her wandering thoughts, she turned her head towards the window, against which the snow still clung. As she watched she became certain that snow was, in fact, still falling, although, through the feathered and frosted glass, it was difficult to be sure. Curiosity overcoming her general feeling of weariness,

Amanda crept out of bed towards the window. No one had arrived yet with the promised refreshment. Whatever this woman's virtues, swiftness was apparently not one of them.

Once across the room, Amanda rubbed her small nose against the pane, as she had often done as a child, and looked out. She had been right. It was snowing, but the wind had died down and the flakes were falling gently, softly beautiful, making whiter the already white world outside. Glancing at the sky, she noted the heavy, overcast grey which seemed to promise ignominiously that there was more bad weather to come. Helplessly Amanda shuddered in spite of having always loved storms such as this. It was nice, she supposed, on picture postcards, or when one was a child, but right now she would have been happier with rain. Down below her window there had obviously been a track of sorts dug out to the drive entrance, but otherwise she could see no sign of any road being properly cleared. Beyond the drive, over the silent white distances, she could discern no movement of any kind. Nothing to indicate there was another soul in the world besides herself. Not anything, even in the immediate vicinity of the house, to be seen!

With one last despairing shudder Amanda turned from the wintry scene and, vaguely uneasy, went back to bed. She was a prisoner—this much was clearly apparent. A prisoner of circumstances and her own folly, and there seemed nothing she could do about it. Weakly she lay back, pulling the warm blankets up over her cold body, pushing back her heavy, silken hair from her pleated forehead, still feeling extraordinarily tired. When the woman did arrive with her tea she would ask her not to disturb her for the remainder of the day. All she wanted to do, she would tell her, was to sleep and sleep.

# CHAPTER THREE

Two days later Amanda was up, feeling much better. She knew it as soon as she woke that morning. Frost and snow still sparkled on her window, but the sun was shining, and in place of her former weariness was a surprising feeling of well-being.

Her jeans and shirt, she saw, had been freshly laundered and placed neatly on top of a small chest of drawers. Relieved that they hadn't been relegated to the dustbin, or left forgotten at the bottom of some laundry-basket, Amanda scrambled quickly out of bed and put them on. Carefully she folded the man-size pyjamas she had been wearing with a mixture of despair and relief. She did have one pair of her own in her rucksack, and wondered where on earth they could be. She must remember to ask Mrs Drew.

Usually so quick in her movements as she was, it took Amanda quite a time to tidy her room and make her bed. She was puzzled and not a little dismayed to find her legs still shaky, and that the slightest exertion brought the dampness of perspiration to her face. In the end she confessed herself unequal to the task, and, vaguely unsatisfied with her endeavours, decided to venture downstairs. There didn't appear to be anyone about, but she could see.

She was a stranger in a strange house. A house, it seemed of some size, with many confusing turnings. Eventually it was the smell of bacon frying which took her unerringly to the kitchen and Mrs Drew.

Mrs Drew was busy at the sink and threw Amanda a rather startled glance over her shoulder as the girl stood uncertainly in the doorway. 'Are you sure you should be up?' she asked bluntly, but with some concern. 'I did think yesterday that you looked better, but I'm not sure that Mr Jason will approve.'

'I'm much better, thank you, Mrs Drew,' Amanda smiled,

ignoring what the woman said about Jason as she gazed about her curiously. For a lone man Jason Meade did himself well! No old-fashioned country kitchen this, but a modern, fitted apartment, light, bright and spacious. A connoisseur's kitchen, all elegant chrome and gleaming tiles. A positive housewife's dream. And overall such glorious warmth, in direct contrast to the bitter cold outside. It must cost quite a packet to centrally heat a house this size. If nothing else, Amanda concluded, with a wry grimace, Mr Meade must be a man of some means!

'You'll have to be careful, of course,' Mrs Drew was advising. 'A proper nasty dose you had an' no mistake!'

'But I'm young and strong and I'll soon get over it,' Amanda rejoined haphazardly, her mind still on Jason Meade's kitchen. The kitchen in the flat had amounted to little more than a box, and the one in the house which the Randalls had rented in America had scarcely been much better. How exciting to work in one such as this! Amanda didn't think she was very domesticated, but her fingers itched suddenly to try out the superb-looking electric cooker. 'You don't have to worry about me, Mrs Drew,' she added, as the woman seemed to be waiting expectantly for something more, 'I can look after myself.'

'That's as maybe, but you'll have to take care.'

'Of course . . .' Amanda smiled again quickly. She had no wish to upset the admirable Mrs Drew who had been so very kind to her. Her smooth brow wrinkled thoughtfully. Somewhere, in the confusion of the last few days, she seemed to remember Jason stating that Mrs Drew was a bit of a tyrant. She couldn't think how he had come by the notion. Of course she might have been mistaken. She had been confused a lot as she had lain in bed. There had been times when she had wanted to get up—when she had actually tried to get up, only to find the room whirling strangely around her. Then strong hands had held her down, gripping the soft flesh of her arms, hurting almost, until she stopped struggling and went back to sleep again. Surely Mrs Drew's hands didn't have that exact firmness, nor her voice the same deep, soothing tones?

As if to confirm her fears, Mrs Drew seemed disposed to talk. 'Mr Jason's looked after you like a mother while you've been ill. I may be speaking out of turn, but I do hope you'll remember to thank him. There were times when you were quite delirious and it took all his strength to hold you down. And him supposed to be on holiday, an' all.'

'On holiday?' Amanda blinked, startled. Why should he be on holiday? Wasn't he a farmer? And surely farmers didn't take holidays in weather like this? He could, of course, be a business man having a winter break. Why hadn't she thought of it? But when she asked Mrs Drew, the good lady shook her head.

'You'd better ask Mr Jason yourself, dear. I only live here with my husband who looks after Mr Jason's stable. I only come in here occasionally when Mr Jason is at home, which isn't very often in the summer.'

'Oh, I see . . .' Amanda didn't, but wasn't sure if it would be circumspect to say so. She wasn't sure if it would be wise to admit she knew little about Jason Meade, or his movements. It might not do to tell Mrs Drew that, until she had arrived in the storm, she hadn't even known such a person existed. Nor did she have any idea how much Jason had told Mrs Drew. It was all too confusing! Perhaps it might have been better if she had waited before coming to the kitchen.

Now she stood frowning uncomfortably, and was unable to suppress a start of relief when Jason Meade spoke coolly behind her.

'Miss Smith will have breakfast with me this morning, Mrs Drew. I have things to discuss with her.'

Amanda turned, somewhat startled. She hadn't heard his approach and her eyes swung curiously to his feet, to the thick grey socks he wore beneath tough cord trousers. His wellingtons he must have discarded, not bothering to replace them with anything else. Never before had she had breakfast with a man in stockinged feet!

Slightly amused, his eyes rested on her uncertain face and

42

she guessed he had read her thoughts. 'You've been out?' she asked hastily, and rather inanely, as with a swift smile at Mrs Drew she followed him from the room.

'Clever girl,' he murmured companionably, taking her arm and guiding her easily, his fingers firm beneath her elbow. 'It's not often one discovers a girl with such powers of deduction, especially on one's own doorstep.'

'You didn't find me on your doorstep,' she retorted, stung by his sarcasm but unable to ignore it, while her senses screamed for her to do just that. 'You hauled me here unconscious.'

'But Mrs Drew doesn't know that.'

'You mean ...' Halfway into the dining room Amanda stopped, almost wrenching her arm from his detaining fingers. She stared at him, catching the deeply green gaze and holding it. 'You mean,' she continued, 'that Mrs Drew actually imagines I was caught in the storm and came here looking for shelter?'

'Right first time! The girl really has brains.' There was a carelessly jeering note in his voice which Amanda hated. He did seem in a mood this morning! The devilish glint was back in his eyes again, his darkness accentuated by the heavy line of his brows.

Colour swept into her face. 'Would she believe you?'

'Why not? People do get lost in these parts, only they're usually men, and at other times of the year.'

'Then it's not exactly unusual?' Amanda stepped further into the elegantly furnished room and perched herself uncomfortably on the edge of the chair he drew out for her with a studious politeness.

'Dartmoor,' he replied, as he seated himself opposite, 'is a lady of many moods, and none of them particularly trustworthy. It has three hundred square miles or so of desolate moorland, beautiful at times beyond words, but strangely capricious. Glorious, many would tell you, on a summer's day, but a devil incarnate in weather like this. It's scarcely the most popular form of amusement, rescuing fair maidens in distress, and it does add to the hazards of winter.'

'You're joking!' Amanda's clear, attractive voice was sullen as she stared mutinously down at her plate.

'Maybe I am,' his glance was enigmatical, 'but I can be as serious as you like. I can't tell how concerned you are about your reputation. You might be a ship passing in the night, but the past has a funny way of catching up. Mrs Drew doesn't know you arrived the evening before she did. I told her, for my sins, that I'd found you in an outhouse at daybreak—a slight deviation from the truth, but it may suffice.'

Amanda flushed as he leant across to fill her cup, the cloudy aroma of the coffee hovering sardonically between them. There was a funny, pulsating little silence which she found impossible to break. One hand crept to her throat in a surge of bewildered embarrassment even while she told herself to be sensible and forget the whole thing. The fact that it was this man who had removed her wet clothing was surely nothing to get in such a state about! He might easily have been a doctor, and it had been the only sensible thing to do. Yet the thought of his hands on her body suffused the whole of it with heat. A flame, which she had never known before, coursed through her, leaving her curiously weak and shaken.

Her eyes jerked to his as she heard the patient note of irony in his voice. 'Stop worrying about yourself, Miranda. The female form when half frozen and wet through doesn't interest me at all. For what it's worth you could try looking at it this way. It was imperative that your clothes were removed and you were in no fit state to do it yourself. I'm not sure now that I wouldn't have left them on if I'd guessed you were such a little prude.'

Not prepared of a sudden to be reasonable, or to forgive that remark, she said sharply, 'You've done nothing but dig at the state of my morals ever since I came here. Why didn't you send right away for Mrs Drew? It might have saved you an awful lot of bother.'

'It might indeed,' he grinned mockingly, 'had I but known Mrs Drew was available. She was supposed to be

44

visiting her sister, nor was it actually her fault that she wasn't. Her husband, whom you've not met, was to have driven her to the station, but unfortunately one of my horses went sick and he wouldn't leave the beast. I could have taken her myself, had I known, but I was away that afternoon and knew nothing of this until the next morning, when, I might add, I was delighted when Tom told me Mrs Drew was still here.'

Not wholly convinced, Amanda countered a little wildly, 'There's still the taxi driver! You seem to have forgotten about him. He knew exactly what time I arrived.'

Abruptly he cut her off with one of his imperious gestures. 'I was coming to that. I distinctly recall several times when he referred to you as a young lad, so there's absolutely no reason why he should connect his passenger with my Miranda Smith. In the first place he only rang because he knows I'm keeping an eye on Combe Farm while the owner and his wife are away. You're not the first intruder I've been informed about, nor likely to be the last. If this man should be in touch with me again, I will simply tell him I failed to find any trace of you, but such an incident is so commonplace, I doubt if he will.'

'You're doing an awful lot to safeguard my reputation!' Confused, Amanda concentrated on the green and gold dining room, striving for breath. That he called her his Miranda was probably only a figure of speech, yet such a lot of what he said made her feel helplessly uncomfortable, sent cold shivers racing down her neck. If he ever discovered her true identity, then heaven help her, one day!

He laughed ironically, his white teeth glinting. 'Why should I bother about your reputation, Miss Miranda? Maybe it's my own I'm worried about.'

This was too much! She released a long-pent-up breath. He couldn't be serious! And yet ... She frowned doubtfully as Mrs Drew came in carrying bacon and eggs. There could be some woman somewhere who might be upset to know what had actually happened. Women, she suspected, so far as Jason Meade was concerned, had their uses, but there might be one whom he regarded in a different light from any other. One woman whose respect and admiration he craved. Not anyone like herself or Veronica, whom he might enjoy teasing. Considering this, as Mrs Drew fussed around the breakfast table, a strange depression settled which she couldn't account for.

When Mrs Drew departed, having satisfied herself they had everything they required, Amanda thrust such unreasonable thoughts from her mind and stated with a touch of sheer bravado, 'I'm feeling much better this morning, Mr Meade. Quite well enough to leave, in fact, so all your well-meant evasions are a waste of time. I'll get away directly after breakfast.'

'How?' His green eyes were coolly sceptical between thick, dark, almost feminine lashes.

'Well ...' Her eyes met his briefly, faintly hostile, yet unable to contain that momentary hard contact. 'By road, I suppose. I won't even bother you for a lift.'

'Such brave independence!' He leant towards her, coffee cup in hand, sharp, sardonic humour about his wryly tilted mouth. 'As the roads are still full of snow you wouldn't get far, I'm afraid. And as I haven't time to rescue you again I suggest you content yourself at Merington until our climate improves.'

'Merington?' Amanda's glance lifted quickly. 'This is the name of your house?'

'My house and small estate, which comprises briefly this house and one farm. The farm I rent out. I have a very good tenant.'

Amanda's spine pricked and tautened defensively. His tone stated clearly that he hoped he had relieved her curiosity, but she had only asked the name of his house! She had no wish to be informed of his business, always supposing one rented farm was all it amounted to, which she doubted! Coolly she brushed back a tangle of hair and reverted to their former conversation. 'Don't ploughs, or whatever is used now to clear snow, still operate in this district?'

His dark face registered only a mild dryness. 'My dear girl,' he murmured smoothly, 'to begin with, my drive is private and almost a mile in length. On top of this, owing, I believe, to the present state of the economy, byroads are not being cleared unless absolutely necessary. Unfortunately, as the telephone wires have also succumbed to the elements, I was unable to explain to anyone about your sore head or my sick horse, but as you've both apparently recovered, it seems I no longer have a case.'

'What I'm trying to say . . .' Amanda began stiffly.

'Just forget it,' he clamped down impatiently, his dark, level glance perfectly hard and steady. 'No amount of argument will make any difference at the moment. Besides,' his eyes ran over her so directly that inexplicably her whole body tingled, 'what strength do you have right now? Just out of bed after a bad dose of 'flu, how far do you imagine you'd get? As a matter of fact I doubt your good sense in getting up this morning, and I definitely forbid you to even think of leaving the house!'

'You couldn't stop me!'

'Don't repeat yourself, Miranda. Just try it and see.'

Staring sullenly at her toast which was all she could manage, she turned her head swiftly to look at him, feeling hot and discomfited, at a definite disadvantage. His voice held hard menace, and his dark head added to the picture, too devastating to challenge. 'All right!' she very nearly hissed at him, her wide blue eyes brightly antagonistic. 'But you might regret not letting me go!'

'Before I let you go, Miranda, you'll see a doctor and have an X-ray, just to make sure everything is all right. Does it still hurt?' he inquired suavely. 'Your head, I mean?'

'No, not really.' Surprise threaded her voice as she touched the tender spot with her fingers, vowing silently that wild horses wouldn't drag her to any hospital with Jason Meade. 'I'm sure you're worrying unnecessarily,' she said. 'I certainly haven't fractured my skull, if that's what you think?'

'I'm not qualified to think anything, Miranda, neither are

you, but I do have my share of common sense. Besides, it could be argued that it was my fault you fell from that ladder.'

'And you do take your responsibilities seriously, Mr Meade.' Her eyes widened innocently, sweeping his face. 'But then a man like you would.'

'I'm overcome.' The look he slanted her was vividly mocking. 'One of these days, Miranda, you'll land in trouble with your wild little tongue. Another man might not be so tolerant.'

She was breathless all of a sudden, nervous enough to glance away. That could mean other things! There was an odd inflection in his voice which she couldn't begin to dissect. Belatedly she tried to salvage a little poise. 'What I said was on the level, Mr Meade. You don't have to look for hidden meanings.'

'I take it, then, that you mean to flatter me?' He smiled in a leisurely way. 'Perhaps we might both learn to understand each other better, Miranda, given time.'

Carefully Amanda lowered her lashes, a pulse in her throat jerking painfully for no reason she could think of. How could she hope to cope with sarcasm so blatant? As soon as the weather cleared she would be gone. They had no time, and he knew it.

Seeking desperately for a safer topic, she asked impulsively, 'If I'm not to go out this morning, what would you suggest I do?'

'You never stop trying, do you?' His gaze slid consideringly to her mutinous mouth. 'You can amuse yourself in the library. There's a TV and enough books to see you through several winters. Unless, of course, you don't read. Today young people seldom do.'

Amanda's blue eyes darkened coldly. 'You talk as though I'm just out of the schoolroom!'

'Not long out, I should say. How old are you, Miranda?'

'Old enough . . .' she replied reluctantly, her brow knitted with delicate uncertainty.

'I asked you a question, Miranda! That's no sort of an

answer!' There was about him a barely suppressed male impatience.

'Rescuing me doesn't give you automatic rights! You don't have to know everything about me!' Amanda's eyes flashed with indignation and a certain wariness, remembering too late what he had said about her tongue. But even in simple questions there could be danger. This man was too astute by far!

If he was aware of the wariness, the stubborn set of soft lips, he took no notice. 'Miranda?' he prompted gently.

'Oh, twenty, if you really must know!' Without notable grace, she jumped to her feet, leaving untouched her second cup of coffee. 'If you'll excuse me,' she added, tossing her head like an obstinate child, 'I think I'll take your advice and read some books. At least they can't lecture and probe!'

But having the last word, Amanda found, wasn't a very satisfactory business. For the remainder of that day and most of the next she saw very little of Jason Meade. In the library she played records and watched the snow-clad moors outside. Preoccupied with her thoughts, she found she couldn't settle to a book, although the deep armchairs by the fire were inviting.

The loss of her shoulder-bag still worried her greatly, but the contents she considered so lethal she dared not mention it again. Sitting by the fire, piecing together as best she could the curious happenings of that momentous night, she came at last to the conclusion that she must have dropped it in the lane at Combe Farm. Vaguely, now, she seemed to recall falling into some kind of ditch. If she was unable to search for it herself, there was at least some comfort to be derived from the fact that as long as the snow lay, her bag would be covered and her secret safe. Safer than herself, perhaps, beneath the predatory male gaze of Jason Meade! The thought came entirely out of the blue, completely unfounded, and for a moment Amanda had the grace to feel ashamed. Yet such thoughts came unbidden, bringing a tremulous excitement, a depth of response, quite foreign to anything she had known before. Jason Meade was quite a

49

man, she had to admit it! Apart from his hard good looks, he was full of domineering authority and polished sophistication. Never in a hundred years would she find enough experience to cope with a man like that, yet for an instant, on a wave of inexplicable longing, she wished she had!

A log on the fire flared, bursting into a shower of sparks before burning itself out in the grate. Unconsciously Amanda shuddered. Such thoughts as she had been thinking were crazy. She must be mad! Perhaps she should have her head examined, as Jason had suggested. The blow she had sustained when she fell must have affected her reasoning and her senses as well. Jason Meade was not for her, nor did she really want him. If some vagrant part of her was clamouring for amorous amusement, then she must look elsewhere!

In the meantime, such ridiculous notions aside, to stay here was probably as convenient as anywhere else—until the family came home. With Mrs Drew and her husband she was adequately chaperoned. Then surely she could quite easily escape and return to Combe Farm. Jason Meade need never know what had become of her, and, because of his doubtful opinion of her, she didn't think he would try to find out.

If he did visit Combe Farm she must endeavour to keep out of his way. He would probably never connect Richard Trent's retiring young daughter with Miranda Smith, and besides, in no time at all she would be gone. It would be sensible to return to London, to stay in some cheap digs and take a training of some sort. It shouldn't be too difficult with a little patience.

Come tea-time on the following afternoon, Amanda discovered that patience was a commodity she seemed short of. Used as she had been during the last two years to leading an outdoor life, to be confined to the house she found extremely tedious. The ache in her limbs appeared to have gone completely, and apart from a slight lassitude she was beginning to feel quite fit again—so much so that she began to resent being ignored by Jason, whom she hadn't seen all day!

Neglect, she decided, was what it amounted to, and as she sat at the kitchen table sharing a pot of tea with Mrs Drew she was unable to resist asking her where he could be. 'Surely, in this weather,' she said, 'he can't find a lot to do outside. I hope he's not staying out because of me?'

It was indiscreet, she knew, to air her feelings so indiscriminately, and she wasn't surprised to find Mrs Drew frowning disapprovingly and shaking her head. 'There's an awful lot to do in weather like this, Miranda! Why, they've hardly stopped for more than a sandwich and a glass of beer since dawn. Snow makes a lot of extra work anywhere, but in no place more so than a stable. My husband Tom could never have managed on his own. Mr Jason knows everything there is to know about horses, and he doesn't believe in wasting time.'

Amanda, who knew nothing about horses, apart from the little she had picked up in Florida when the twins had developed a sudden urge to ride, felt unable to argue with Mrs Drew's apparently logical statements. 'I'm afraid I'm not a country girl,' she smiled, 'but I'm going to borrow a pair of gumboots and go and see for myself. Otherwise I'm going to die of boredom more easily than the 'flu.'

Mrs Drew heaved a huge, sceptical sigh which Amanda pretended not to hear as she turned and ran upstairs to fetch her jacket. Her feet skipped the wide staircase, the animation which lifted her spirits at the thought of being out touching her face, bringing fresh colour to her pale cheeks. Mrs Drew might not approve, nor might Jason, but fresh air, Amanda felt sure, couldn't do her any harm. It was probably what she needed after being cooped up for so long.

Outside it was colder than she had expected and she thought longingly of the thick coat packed with the rest of her clothes at the flat. The thin jerkin she wore provided little protection against the frost and snow, and she felt annoyed with herself again for not bringing something warmer. Even if she had managed to break into Combe

Farm, she might have known what to expect on Dartmoor!

Away from the immediate vicinity of the house, Amanda turned her attention to the drive. There was no one about, no one to stop her escaping, but she saw at once that there would be no need. As Jason had pointed out, the road was full of snow, and there seemed no sign yet of a thaw setting in. After a few minutes of ploughing through the frozen waste she gave up, leaning against a small, upright piece of fencing until she regained her breath, staring out across the countryside. In the late afternoon sunshine the snow and frost sparkled and glistened, turning the moors and fells into a miniature Antarctic, desolate and grim, yet fairy-like in its gleaming whiteness—a remote, treeless wilderness, somewhere Amanda had read, and, looking over Dartmoor now, she was inclined to believe it. A wild waste of granite and bog, guarded by grim tors, that bowed to neither man nor beast! With a mild shudder Amanda turned away. She was getting too fanciful; it must be the atmosphere of the place! She must go and find Jason Meade. The human elements might be easier to deal with.

Merington, she noticed as she struggled back, was a rambling old house, as cosy-looking outside as it was in—cosy by contrast with the Moor, at any rate. The low, deep-set windows and square, squat chimneys looked as if they had withstood the storms of centuries, and the thick belt of Scots pines behind it provided a protective barrier between the house and the barren lands beyond. What sort of a man was Jason Meade to live here by choice? Amanda wondered, as she ploughed around the corner of the copse. At times, during winters like this, the loneliness must be almost too great to be endured. Again curiosity beset her as to his real profession. He wasn't just a country landlord, of that she was certain.

The afternoon was wearing on before Amanda reached the stables. She found them by following a roughly hewn track through a collection of old, apparently unused buildings and through another thick belt of trees into a field.

Here, to her surprise, she saw that the snow had been cleared from paths and yards, to make an area where horses would be able to exercise comparatively easily. The stables seemed quite extensive, well kept by any standards, this much was clearly obvious in spite of the snow, but of Jason Meade there was no sign. She must just look and see.

She turned, the sun, settling almost to the horizon, slanting into her eyes and nearly blinding her. When she did manage to focus, she found herself staring straight at him as he emerged from a doorway on her right.

'What the devil are you doing here?' he exclaimed, his voice flat and hard, not in the least welcoming.

She spun her head a little from side to side, dazed by his unexpected appearance, even though she had known he must be around. Why, when she saw him, did her legs turn curiously weak, and her pulses jerk in such a crazy fashion? There was even a familiar faintness creeping over her which she could never account for!

Then he was towering in front of her, brilliant impatient eyes travelling over her with intense irritation, noting the tumbled bare head, the peculiar intensity of her face with its marked pallor. 'You little fool!' His hard, lean fingers gripped her arms, shaking her none too gently. 'Didn't I tell you to stay inside? I've enough on here without you adding to my worries!'

The faintness passed—it was probably the impact of brutal fingers and hard-hitting words which sobered her immediately. 'I don't intend adding to your troubles,' she choked. 'I came to see if I could help!' Which wasn't exactly the truth, but the truth would never suffice. What tolerance would he have with a girl who had only been looking for air?

'Help!' His hands tightened compulsively as his jaw clamped. 'Help with what, might I ask? You're swaying around like a leaf in the wind, not yet recovered from a bad dose of 'flu.'

A tremor ran through her, but she beat it down. 'You accused me only yesterday of repeating myself, Mr Meade!'

'I don't want any backchat from you, Miranda!' His dark face was sardonic, and the colour mounted beneath her skin. 'I'm going to send you back to the house.'

'Please, Jason ...'

'Jason ...' His voice mocked her, yet changed slightly, subtly. 'I was wondering when you'd get around to it.'

'I'm sorry—I didn't mean ...' She trailed off helplessly. Why should she be apologising for using his name when he had been using hers freely?

'Don't apologise, Miranda, I like it. It puts our relationship on an entirely different footing.'

Amanda blinked, her blue eyes darkening, staring up into his. There was some kind of laughter beating in his voice which she didn't begin to understand. The impatience had gone, at least momentarily; even the grip of his fingers slackened, became gentle. Yet none of this did she find reassuring, and her thick lashes flickered and came down. 'I don't really think it makes much difference,' she replied carefully.

'Don't you, Miranda?' His hands slid away, and his laughter was hard and brief and his eyes rested on the full curve of her mouth. 'All the difference in the world, I should think, but we'll see, my little waif.' One arm came up and curved around her shoulders as he turned her. 'Come and see my horses if you must, but don't be too keen to offer assistance. In weather like this I'm hard put to it to resist a helping hand—or anything else, for that matter.'

There was an odd, disturbing look on his face that flicked tiny tremors down her spine, sent sharp warning signals along her nerves which she was rash enough to ignore. He enjoyed taunting and teasing, but it would mean little. Possibly the sudden spell of bad weather had stirred a devil in him. Many men looked for scapegoats when overworked. If she could in any way relieve his feelings, then it might repay in some measure that which she owed him.

That evening Jason took her on a personally conducted tour of his stables, and all the next day Amanda worked by his side, her renewed offer of assistance accepted. In a few

54

short hours his horses became a delight, a nameless terror; the pleasure of hands sliding down warm skin; the wonderful release of an all-enveloping hug when Jason was looking the other way. He didn't altogether approve, and she found herself resentful when he said she was too impulsive, when he warned her of the perils and none of the pleasures. The huge chestnut gelding she steered clear of, fastidious and thoroughbred though he might be. A big dapple-grey she eyed warily also, but there were others, many others. One especially, a little chestnut filly, perfect in every detail, she liked very much, and would have given much to possess.

'You could hunt that one well.' Jason, catching her in the throes of ecstatic contemplation, passed the remark dryly.

Startled out of her reverie, Amanda glanced around at him. She was supposed to be spreading fresh straw, a lighter job which was all he would allow. She hadn't heard his approach. Now, flushing slightly, she considered what he said. 'I shouldn't want to hunt. I've never liked the sound of it.'

'Well, we certainly don't need to agree on that controversial subject.' His eyes glinted derisively, warning her subtly that, while tolerant, he would be in no way receptive to her views.

Stung, Amanda tossed her dark head. 'I don't even ride.'

'I could always teach you.' That and more, his eyes promised.

Again she experienced a tremor in her stomach—the feeling that she was falling through space. She said breathlessly, without thinking, 'I tried once and fell off. I don't have the aptitude.'

'You could be surprised,' his smile glinted whitely. 'I believe otherwise. You certainly have the right approach, which my horses appear to appreciate. Anyone else would have been trampled underfoot long ago. Have you ever worked in a stable, Miranda?'

'If I had I should have learnt to ride.'

'You wouldn't fancy it? Tom isn't as young as he used to be, and he could do with some help. You might do worse,'

55

he added with gentle emphasis.

She moved her head fretfully, evading that brilliant green glance. 'Is that an invitation, Mr Meade?'

'Jason,' he corrected softly. 'It might be a more rewarding existence than wandering footloose.'

'A sort of rehabilitation centre?'

'You said that, Miranda, not I. I'm not interested in the young, generally, or the saving of their tender skins.'

'You can be quite brutal when you choose, Mr Meade!' Resentfully she dug her hands into the pockets of the fur-lined coat he had loaned her. It was huge, far too big, but it was warm and the fur collar caressed her smooth cheeks snugly.

His eyes swept her face, the creamy skin. 'Now what's that supposed to mean?'

'Oh, never mind, but I'm afraid I can't accept your offer.' She moved back tensely. 'It would never work out.'

She retreated, but he was quicker, and she shivered uncontrollably as his hand grasped her shoulder, closing painfully over the bone. 'You don't believe in giving yourself a chance, do you, Miranda? What I'm offering might not be the ultimate, but you would never need to go hungry or penniless again.'

'What you're offering, Mr Meade, could be just as questionable. I should hate to merely change one form of bondage for another.'

His tingling grip tightened with disturbing intimacy. 'There are lots of things, Miranda, I might be fully justified in pointing out, only politeness and something else, which I can't quite clearly define, holds me back. But before you so rashly discard my offer you'd be well advised to think it over. Such an opportunity might not come again.'

The hard edge to his voice bothered her and she looked away, her fingers clenching. 'Some things,' she said swiftly, 'are better not considered. Instinctively one knows.'

'Because instinctively one suspects the worst,' he mocked, his expression dark, his eyes immobile on her set face. 'Don't you realise how like you're getting to a small wild animal, afraid to trust anything or anyone any more?'

Her hand moved up convulsively to push past him. 'Your horses are nice, Mr Meade, but not for me. That's all there is to it. You exaggerate the rest. Now, if you don't mind, I'm going to help Mrs Drew with dinner. I promised, in case you're thinking I'm running away!'

'Now why ever should I think that, young lady?' An enigmatic smile played about his mouth. 'You couldn't run far in this weather anyway. Go and assist Mrs Drew by all means. I'll be in for dinner this evening and shall expect you to join me. I have another proposition which you might find more interesting than my stables.'

Amanda walked away from him, along the snow-cleared path back to the house. He was used to being obeyed, but the thought of having dinner with him filled her with a tremulous apprehension. He seemed very keen that she should stay where he could keep an eye on her. How much longer, she wondered, could she hold out against him?

# CHAPTER FOUR

While Mrs Drew appreciated Amanda's help in the kitchen, she noticed the girl looked tired, and when the casserole was simmering gently in the oven she advised her to go to her room and rest.

'Lie on your bed and close your eyes for an hour, my dear, otherwise Mr Jason will be after me for working you too hard. He won't want to look at a pale face throughout dinner.'

Reluctantly, if not altogether unwillingly, Amanda agreed, although about dining with Jason she was full of reservations. 'I really think I should have mine in here with you, Mrs Drew. I'm not very suitably dressed for the dining room. I have only these trousers which I've worn continually.'

'Mr Jason usually changes.' Doubtfully Mrs Drew nodded, glancing at Amanda's denim-clad legs, her slight frown indicating that she agreed in some measure with what Amanda had said. 'It would have been better if you'd had a nice dress,' she added thoughtfully. 'There are some dresses belonging to Mr Jason's sister who's abroad at the moment with her husband. Miss Alison had far more dresses than she knows what to do with, and I'm sure she wouldn't mind your borrowing one for the evening, especially as you're both much the same size, but I'm afraid it's not for me to suggest it, and, being a man, it probably wouldn't occur to Mr Jason.'

'Oh, no, please don't say anything!' Amanda smiled, yet grew hot when she thought of what Jason might think. He might imagine she was dressing up for his benefit, and she certainly didn't want him to think that! 'It was nice of you to worry about me,' she went on quickly, 'but the storm will soon be over and I'll be gone. My pants will just have to hold out a little longer, that's all.'

Mrs Drew sighed. 'Tom was just saying that the wind is changing. The snow could all be away, come morning.'

'By morning?' Abruptly, on her way to the door, Amanda jerked to a halt. 'As quickly as that, Mrs Drew?'

'Quite easily. With the wind in the right direction.'

Mrs Drew obviously spoke from experience, yet doubtfully Amanda remained frowning. 'It doesn't seem possible. Doesn't it cause flooding, Mrs Drew?'

'Sometimes—sometimes not,' Mrs Drew shrugged. 'There's nothing so strange as weather. I've seen snow disappear, almost without a trace, you might say. Dartmoor is full of rivers and streams, but fortunately we aren't on a river here. Now take Combe Farm, for instance, what Mr Jason is keeping an eye on while his friends are away. They sit nearly on top of a river and sometimes, in a flood, the water comes almost up to the door.'

'Combe Farm?' Amanda heard herself repeating stupidly.

'Yes. That and the river about four miles away, so we're quite safe here.'

'I see . . .' Nervously Amanda probed, unaware that she was giving the wrong impression. 'Is that as the crow flies—the four miles, I mean?'

'Well, yes, I suppose so. You turn right at the end of the drive and the road runs straight. But you don't need to worry, dear,' the housekeeper smiled reassuringly. 'We're too high up at Merington to be in danger.'

'Of course not,' said Amanda, escaping.

As she ran up to her room she took Mrs Drew's advice, throwing herself on to her bed without being fully aware of what she was doing. If the snow was to go through the night, then so must she! It wouldn't do to be caught unprepared, but the idea of sneaking out like a fugitive in the early hours was curiously daunting. She even knew a peculiar reluctance to leave Merington at all. In the few short days that she had been here she had formed a surprising attachment for the place, foolish perhaps when she had known she must leave. Strange fancies crowded through her head. Why not make a clean breast of everything, and beg Jason to let her stay and help with his horses! It would be a job, and one which immediately appealed to her. Perhaps she might live with the Drews, in their cottage, or even cycle over each day from Combe Farm?

Such a notion, however, she squashed almost before it was born. By setting up a fabrication of fictitious stories she had burnt her boats too badly ever to hope to get away with such an idea. Jason, if he was ever to discover the truth, would never forgive her. No man, however indifferent, enjoyed being made a fool of. And as for the family at Combe Farm, Richard and Eva almost certainly wouldn't approve!

With a sigh Amanda turned, burying her hot face against her pillows, admitting that she was drawn to Jason Meade in some comprehensible way, and instinctively sensing that he was not indifferent to her. Why, she could not even begin to guess. As quickly as she had flopped down on to her bed, she rolled off it to scramble across the floor to consider herself in the dressing-table mirror. She saw that since her illness she looked as thin as a cat, but with huge blue eyes instead of green, gleaming with the desperation of the homeless. Yet her thinness, and perhaps the shirt which appeared to have shrunk since Mrs Drew dried it, did nothing to hide the taut curves of her body, lending a certain provocative mystery to her fine-boned face, adding sensuous shadows about her high cheekbones and mouth, physical features which she noted without being fully able to assimilate. What, she wondered, seeing only a complete lack of glamour, would any man see in her? True, she had known few very well. There had been Herman—not that she considered Jason in any way like him. Jason, she felt sure, would never attempt to assault her! He might acknowledge that he wanted her, but would apply more finesse. With him there would be no clumsy fumblings in a bathroom, but might he not get what he wanted in the end? Possibly, of the two, Jason would be the more dangerous, and she mustn't allow a different approach to blind her to the fact.

She could find nothing in the mirror to convince her she was irresistible, but men were surely creatures of some promiscuity. Many, she admitted, striving honestly, would consider a wandering girl like herself as fair game. If Jason Meade thought of her in this way, then it would be up to her to correct such an impression, but she doubted if he ever thought of her at all, apart from the odd moment when she happened to cross his path.

Impatiently she turned away from her reflection in the glass. There were other things more important than her appearance. A means of escape, for instance! Amanda walked to the window and spent a long time contemplating the night.

She had washed her face and was almost ready to go down when Mrs Drew knocked on the door and looked in. 'Mr Jason says you're to go along to Miss Alison's room and help yourself to anything you like.'

'Oh, Mrs Drew, I told you not to mention it!' Annoyed, Amanda felt swift colour staining her cheeks. This was just the sort of thing she had hoped to avoid.

'I didn't, dear!' Crossly Mrs Drew pursed prim lips. 'When Mr Jason came in he mentioned it himself! I'm too old to bother about such things, or for running upstairs for that matter,' she added breathlessly.

Suitably chastised, Amanda flushed deeper. 'I'm sorry, Mrs Drew, but you shouldn't have bothered to come up. I really don't need a dress or anything else, as I told you before.'

'Well, when the master makes inquiries, don't forget to tell him I told you!' Mumbling to herself, the woman departed, leaving Amanda staring after her, indignation etched on her face.

'You didn't find anything suitable, I see?' Jason queried, as she ran downstairs.

He was standing in the hall, near the spot where he had been when she had first looked over the balustrade and seen him properly for the first time. On this occasion, it seemed he might almost have been waiting for her. Her eyes went swiftly over him as he stood, immaculate in his dark suit, the light from above him gleaming on black hair, very

61

thick and curling crisply, following the well-shaped line of his head. For all her convincing argument with herself in the bedroom, excitement began to flow through her, lighting her eyes so that they glimmered, reflecting a thousand sapphire stars. Hastily, as she drew nearer, she flickered long lashes, hiding the sudden whirl of her senses, the traitorous pulsing of her heart. Where this man was concerned she must keep a firm grip on herself, his attractiveness would defeat any wavering resolutions.

On reaching the bottom step of the stairs she carefully inclined her small head. 'Thank you,' she answered tonelessly, averting her gaze, 'but I didn't want anything—or need it. What I'm wearing will do quite nicely.'

'You feel comfortable in something you've worn all day?' his voice held only a mild curiosity, yet his eyes, as they went over her, held anything but mildness and stirred her blood, precipitating a need to defend herself.

'I feel more at ease in my own things,' she uttered, feeling at that moment quite the reverse but reluctant to say so.

'Which isn't quite the same thing,' he said shortly, his gaze lingering with a hint of disapproval on her rather creased attire. Once a tramp always a tramp—Amanda decided she read his thoughts quite clearly, and found herself stiffening with resentment. Otherwise, now that he had mentioned his sister's clothes himself, she might have given in gracefully. For a brief second she had been tempted.

Instead she murmured, avoiding his eyes, 'I should be quite happy to have my dinner in the kitchen with the Drews.'

'Happier than having it with me, perhaps. But I don't feel like my own company this evening, Miranda, so you must endure. And as I told you before, I have something to discuss with you. It matters little what you choose to wear.'

There was obviously nothing more to be said. Amanda drew a quick, fortifying breath as she followed him across the hall, studying unobserved the back of his handsome dark head, the unrelenting set of his broad shoulders. As she passed the telephone, she asked without meaning to, 'Has the line been repaired yet? I haven't heard it ringing since I arrived.'

His head inclined slightly so that she saw his hard profile, the ironic tilt of one dark eyebrow. 'As I've been unable to report it out of order, it's scarcely likely.'

'But someone,' she protested, 'could have reported it from outside.'

'Quite possibly, Miranda. Services, in weather like this, can be erratic, and I don't intend to complain. I only know I can't use it.'

'You were using it on the night I arrived!' She had said it once already, yet something inside her forced her to repeat it, a crazy thing to do, because he had been talking to Veronica, and her persistence would almost certainly start him thinking. He was astute enough not to miss a move. Momentarily, however, Amanda was unable to resist it. His relationship with Veronica was beginning to hurt insidiously. Only, Amanda assured herself, because after all the trouble she'd gone to it would be completely illogical if Veronica's marriage was to fail due to another source altogether!

'Someone happened to ring me . . .' As she had feared, his eyes were suddenly sharper as he stood aside to let her pass before him through the dining-room door. 'Afterwards the line went dead. Did you, by any chance, overhear that conversation, Miranda?'

He knew she had, the knowledge was there in the dark, mocking depth of his eyes, and his expression told her to mind her own business! He expected to conduct any number of affairs without implied criticism, while already he had judged and condemned one lone girl without one scrap of concrete evidence!

If she had been lovelier, more experienced, Amanda vowed she would have done her uttermost to attract him, to have made him fall in love with her. It might not have been too difficult if she had been a little more sophisticated, a little more knowledge as to what made a man tick. Then she could have snapped her fingers at him, sent him away with a broken heart, or a degree less assurance. If nothing else it might have served to demonstrate the pain of philandering with the affections of others.

'A penny for them, Miranda? At times you have an infuriating habit of retreating into a world of your own. I asked you a question.'

'I'm sorry ...' Amanda sat down as he pushed her chair beneath her with a punishing little jerk. 'Many things on that particular evening are hazy, Mr Meade. I was only trying to remember.'

'Well, don't strain yourself, my dear,' he replied dryly. Not seating himself immediately, he went to the sideboard, absently contemplating a selection of bottles. 'Would you rather drink Muscadet or a German Riesling perhaps with your smoked salmon? Mrs Drew appears to have excelled herself this evening—or was it you?'

Amanda shook her head, disclaiming any credit. 'Thank you,' she murmured as he waited coolly, his eyes on her face. 'I'll have the Muscadet, but only a little. After being ill too much might go to my head.'

'You didn't guess, did you, Miranda?' Jason carried the bottle to the table, asking the question suavely as he filled her glass. He smiled as he pushed it towards her, and the humorous look came back to his eyes.

Plagued by apprehension, she glanced up sharply. 'What is that supposed to mean? Another black mark, I suppose?'

'Don't be foolish!' He lifted his own drink in a silent toast, faintly mocking. 'You appear to have a one-track mind, but I'm not sure if I follow you.'

'Sorry,' she muttered, without notable grace, unable to return his gesture. 'It doesn't really matter.' Confused, she looked down at her hands, with an effort holding them still on the table. From off them she had washed all signs of her stint in the stables, and her long, slender fingers were smooth if still faintly tanned from her stay in America.

Her hands diverted him, although he sounded vaguely irritated as he reached over and picked one up, his lean fingers closing over hers, turning the palm up and examining it carefully. 'You've rather beautiful hands, Miranda. This tan, which you appear to have all over—where did you come by it? On the Continent?'

'No . . .' She seemed to choke on her breath as, startled, she glanced at him—quickly before averting her eyes. Her all-over tan, he said! Her pulses jerked and the hand he held clenched convulsively. It would have been so easy to tell him—in Florida, playing with the twins! But she couldn't possibly give him even that small detail of information without arousing the suspicions she was so scared of. Which was crazy, really, because Veronica must have sailed yesterday, and if she had any sense she would say so, lightly, making a joke of it. No need to mention Herman. All she need say was that she hadn't wanted to go, and was scared Veronica would make a fuss. But it was far from the simple task she had anticipated. Too much deception lay between herself and this man who held her hand with so light yet so tenuous a grip. Never in a thousand years dared she risk the torrent of furious contempt which would surely pour on her head before her first words were out! Besides, there was always a slim chance that Veronica might not have gone as arranged. Confusion surged, rippling nervously through her slight body. No—she must just wait and disappear. It would be so much easier.

'Just, no?' Startled from her anxious reverie, she became aware of his brilliant gaze whipping across her, and when she flushed unhappily and nodded, he prompted cynically, 'Sometimes, Miranda, I'm convinced you don't know truth from fiction. In my line of business, my dear, I've learnt to recognize a tan which isn't British.'

'Your line of business,' she repeated, the colour coming under her skin as she almost snatched away her hand. Then, in spite of her flash of truculence, she leaned forward, her blue eyes vividly alight. 'You mean, your business apart from the farm?'

'I don't farm, Miranda. I've never pretended to.'

'So you said, but I . . .'

'Never mind,' he interrupted briefly, his smile softly derisive. 'Eat up your dinner—Mrs Drew has left it all on the hotplate. If you like you can serve the casserole, and, afterwards, I'll tell you all about it.'

Mrs Drew's casserole was delicious. They went into the lounge for coffee. 'I use the library mostly, but this makes a change.' Jason poured coffee which was already percolating on a low table before the fire. He didn't attempt to supplement the one side-light which Mrs Drew had apparently switched on, and the room appeared cosy beneath its gentle glow.

Amanda took her coffee with a murmured word of thanks, gazing at the classic marble fireplace, the exquisite painting above the mantel of a Victorian lady surrounded by her children and dogs. Her eyes left the painting to take in the elegance of the room, the gleaming panelling of the walls, the crystal wall lights, the superb, silky-looking carpet, the pictures hung against soft green wallpaper. The button-back chair she sat in was covered in soft blue and gold, picking up the colours of the carpet, and opposite stood a fine Regency sofa. Another, in gold brocade, was placed on her right, and after pouring his own coffee, Jason lowered on to it his not insubstantial weight.

'Do you like it?' he asked softly, aware of her close surveillance. 'You haven't been in here before?'

She drew a cool, expressive little breath. 'I don't roam uninvited in a house where I'm not even a guest! I like your library, Mr Meade. I've enjoyed playing your records, but I'm afraid I couldn't settle to reading any of your books.'

He grinned for a moment as if her studied little speech amused him, his eyes steady on her flushed young face. 'You find it difficult to settle to anything, perhaps?'

'I would like to train for something,' she retorted swiftly and impulsively. 'If you're referring to a job? I will have to earn my living.'

'One might have thought there were easier ways,' he said lightly, and she bit her full bottom lip painfully, not entirely fooled by the ironic glint in his eyes. When she made no reply he added smoothly, 'Does hotel work appeal to you at all, Miranda?'

'Hotel work?' She moved her tongue quickly over her sore lip, her blue eyes bewildered. 'I'm afraid I've never even thought about it. When I have considered a career it was never to do with people. Animals maybe, or children, but nothing so competitive as working in a hotel.'

'Such work, my dear, is no more competitive than anything else. Besides, you turned down my offer of a job in my stables.'

Amanda sighed, for a moment confused, and put down her coffee cup with a tiny clatter. 'Mr Meade,' she said emphatically, 'you don't have to worry about finding me employment. I'm not your responsibility. All in good time I'll find something myself.'

He ignored this completely. 'I happen to own a string of hotels, many of which suffer to some extent from a shortage of staff. Yes, even in times like these,' he stated, seeing her raised eyebrows, her dubious expression. 'A lot of hotel staff like to move around, and, as much of our work is seasonal, perhaps this is just as well. But I do have places which are open all the year round and it would be quite easy to find you something.'

'Such as . . .?' Why didn't she turn his offer down flat? She felt not one spark of interest, so she assured herself. Why, she would much rather stay and help with his horses —if she had been bound to make a choice, which she wasn't. No, she might as well be honest, if only with herself. The question so glibly on her lips had been prompted more by curiosity than anything else—the fact that she had discovered Jason Meade's occupation, if owning a string of hotels could be described as such !

She heard his relaxed drawl. 'I'm not sure exactly where you'd fit in. I should have to know a little more about you.'

'Then, after I agreed to be interviewed, you'd come to the regretable conclusion that my qualifications are in no way suitable.'

He intercepted her line of thought with trained perception. 'I don't need to know everything about you, Miranda. You have no faith in people.'

Her colour came and ebbed with confusion and she glanced at him sideways, catching his ambiguous gaze. 'A man like you would only need to know so much. You would have no difficulty in putting two and two together.'

'Supplying the deficiencies, you mean?' his voice mocked.

'Whichever way you care to put it.'

He considered her for a long moment from under slanting black brows, his eyes narrowed on her slightly averted face. 'Are you parents still alive, Miranda? I distinctly remember you mentioning your father, as if he at any rate was very much so.'

Amanda's fingers clenched nervously. Did he never miss a thing! 'My parents can be of no interest to you, Mr Meade.' Wildly she answered, not prepared to listen to the small voice of reason which warned her of future recriminations.

'So you refuse to tell me anything? Where you're going, where you've been?'

'The latter could be easier.'

'Not if you'd allow me to help.'

That way could only be dangerous, she knew, but did not say so aloud. Instead she silently shook her silky head. 'You only want to help me because you feel responsible for my tumble off the ladder—you said so yourself. After the snow has gone, and me with it, I doubt if your conscience will continue to trouble you.'

'So we've come to the end of the road, you and I? Or is it, I wonder, just the beginning?'

She moved uneasily in her soft chair, aware that his eyes hadn't moved from her face. 'You don't have to trouble.'

An exasperated sigh escaped his tight lips. 'To be quite frank, Miranda, I'm asking myself, right now, why I bother. My common sense tells me to let you go. And yet ...? Have you ever been intrigued by anyone, Miranda?'

'You, in a way,' Amanda smiled with courageous frankness. 'You say you have hotels, yet you apparently choose to live here by yourself. Why?'

'And she asks, with a rare economy in words!' An amused quirk broke the set contours of his mouth, lightening the brooding glint in his eye. 'It would seem that curiosity can be motivated by entirely different emotions. But do you expect, I wonder, the same sort of answers as you give me?'

Amanda flushed, but before she could speak he went on. 'Don't worry,' he mocked, 'mine is the more generous nature. During summer, Miranda, I have little time to spend here. It's in the winter that I indulge myself by stealing a few weeks at Merington with my horses. In summer I have to ration myself to weekends.'

Amanda's thick lashes flickered. 'But you don't keep any staff? Mrs Drew mentioned that you did most of the work yourself. Wouldn't a smaller place, under the circumstances, have been better?'

'It might, my dear, but Mrs Drew obviously didn't tell you I was left this house, and happen to like it. And to be able to look after myself for a change I consider a very real privilege. As a matter of fact Mrs Drew does come in and tidy me up occasionally, but one lone bachelor doesn't create much work.'

'Your sister ...?'

'Yes, Alison.' One dark eyebrow rose fractionally. 'She and her husband do spend a little time with me.'

And he had accused her of being economical with words!

'It's really a family home,' she mused, unthinking, and went pink with confusion when he added smoothly,

'A house for children.' A slight pause, silence, apart from a rising wind against the window. 'First, Miranda, I should have to find myself a wife. As I've told you before, people around here observe the conventions.'

'I'm surprised you haven't done so before now.' To hide a very real disconcertion the words tripped impulsively off her tongue.

'Perhaps I haven't met the right girl,' he grinned, not obviously put out by Amanda's pertinent question. 'I can assure you that when I do she won't be long in knowing about it.'

A faint shudder traversed the length of Amanda's spine, quivering into definite awareness. In spite of his tolerance something in his voice seemed to hold a soft threat, a hint that she could go so far but no further without some definite retaliation. The cool glitter in his eyes spoke to her, giving emphasis to what he said. If Jason loved a girl what chance would she have of ever escaping?

The faint underlying threat in his voice pinned her to her chair. 'I shouldn't believe in wasting any time, Miranda.'

Curiously at loss for words, conscious of tension in mind and body, she shook her head, her hair, a silken cloud beginning to grow long again, falling across her warm cheeks. Retreating with the wavering instincts of a coward, she said, 'I think I'll go to bed, if you don't mind. The snow seems to have made me tired.'

'Your too recent attack of 'flu, you mean, although being out in the snow could be a contributing factor.'

He spoke brusquely, there was nothing to warn her as she jumped to her feet he would catch hold of her wrist to pull her swiftly against him. 'Poor Miranda,' he murmured, as she jerked against his side, 'did you imagine I would let you escape so easily?'

For one moment, when she might have been free, Amanda was startled, too taken by surprise to move, too shocked to find within herself even the smallest gesture of protest. Tension mounted in her, fine and taut, a prickle of sensitive awareness, while she sought to convince herself that nothing he had said had in any way prepared her for a development like this. His hands slid into the small of her back as he pulled her completely into his arms, his eyes faintly enigmatical. 'Poor Miranda,' he said again, very softly. 'Aren't you even going to struggle?'

For a man whose business was hotels his muscles were surprisingly hard and tough, and there was some violence in the way he drew her to his side. Through her thin shirt she could feel the thump of his heart against her bare skin, and

70

her head spun a little as she quivered from the first shock of reaction. She didn't struggle—she didn't of a sudden want to struggle, a strange sensation of finality subduing any reactionary feelings sweeping over her like a cloud. She couldn't begin to guess why he had pulled her into his arms. Maybe there didn't have to be a reason? Perhaps like Herman he just plainly wanted her, and like Herman he was endeavouring to take what he desired? Yet the thought of this man didn't shock her as Herman had shocked her. Jason was someone entirely different. If he wanted her he might be content at first with kisses, to woo her gently until he was sure she cared enough to give herself completely. With Jason a girl wouldn't need to be scared.

Lost in the extravagance of her thoughts, she gave no indication of having even heard what he said. With a soft sigh she relaxed against him, one hand, seemingly of its own accord, finding its way under his jacket, hugging him to her, finding an exquisite delight in just being near him, allowing totally alien emotions to wash over her, sweeping her up. It was unbelievable, yet utterly magical that anything could be like this!

'Miranda,' his voice was low as his hand slid under her hair, forcing her face up, 'are you telling me the truth about yourself? Girls who wander as you do are not usually without some experience, but how could I ever be sure? You're young and seemingly innocent, yet how could I tell?'

'I don't know . . .' In her drugged state Amanda was scarcely aware of what he was saying, the reply she gave barely more audible than the pulse which beat unevenly at the base of her throat. When he deliberately bent his dark head and put his mouth to it the gasp which escaped her parted lips came more clearly to his ears.

'Miranda,' his voice deepened, thickening slightly as he spoke against her soft skin. 'You're small, so slender, I could crush you. Yet you're all woman, or will be before I'm done with you. You aren't scared of me, are you?'

His arms tightened and a surge of something like flame closed over her, blocking out everything else. What did she

71

care whether he thought her innocent or not? In his arms she had certainly no wish to remain so; the impulse to surrender smouldered in every vein. She drew a soft, shuddery breath and lifted her lips to his, one hand going urgently to his face. When his head came down and he found her mouth, her muffled cry seemed to strike right into him.

To run right through him, as did the way in which she responded to that first touch of his lips, surrendering to his will with compulsive desire, not attempting to hide in any way the complete submission of her body beneath the dominant strength of his. Beneath his mouth her trembling lips parted, quivered in what might have been a soft moan, but he continued to kiss her, pressing her head back into the hard curve of the settee, his hands holding her, arousing in her an ever-increasing response.

'Miranda!' He spoke her name again, then released her lips momentarily while he still held her close, his eyes studying her, oddly hesitant, yet clearly determined, not willing to relinquish an inch what was so nearly within his grasp. 'Miranda,' he said softly, 'you won't have any regrets.'

She stirred, aware that he waited, taking a long time to open her eyes. Never had she known this consuming, intolerable weakness, such burning excitement, such complete indifference to the consequences of her behaviour. Why must he ask questions, expect answers which her feverish mind refused to give, while she only wanted to drift and drift, to allow herself to be consumed by the tumult of her senses.

'Please, Jason,' she whispered, her gaze going no further than his mouth, her heavy lashes falling again as his eyes glittered formidably and he began once more to kiss her, the pressure of his lips on her hot skin bringing a burning delight, an aching desire to belong to him completely. No longer was she Amanda, prudent young daughter of Professor Trent, rather proud of her virtue, but someone entirely different. In Jason Meade's arms her whole preconceived conception of herself was shattered. She was just another woman, seemingly more wanton than most!

Jason kissed her. He heard and understood the wild, sweet longing in her voice and left her in no doubt that he was more than able to furnish all she desired. The pressure of his mouth softened and deepened until reality wasn't there any more, just a high, wild singing in her ears, a thunderous clamouring of emotions.

Then suddenly, as the pressure of his mouth began to change subtly and his arms hurt, a penetrating knocking somewhere in the hall broke through a moment charged with tension. The man lifted his head with a soft exclamation, and Amanda was released, to fall back against the disordered cushions, jerked back rudely to full realization. Horror replaced the sensuous clouds in her eyes as she stared up at Jason. A knock on a door had saved her! This was the only message to register on her numbed brain. Unrealistically Victorian, she could think of nothing else as Jason, after one decisive glance, turned quickly and left the room.

Not waiting to give herself time to think or even to tidy her tumbled hair, Amanda struggled to her feet and rushed after him, the excitement in her veins changing to shame and a sad little fury.

Tom Drew was standing in the hall beside the library door. She heard him explaining to Jason, 'I'm sorry, Mr Meade, I thought you was in here. No wonder I couldn't get you to hear!'

She heard Jason say, 'Well?' tersely.

'It's the little filly, sir,' Tom replied. 'I think she's going to have her foal and I think there could be complications. I'd like you to come and have a look, and I certainly think we'll need the vet.'

Tom's hurried explanation stopped Amanda in her tracks, her startled glance swinging to Jason, her quick compassion for all four-legged animals showing in the anxious concern which widened her shadowed blue eyes. Had Jason forgotten no phone was working? There could be no help in that direction. 'Tom,' she said quickly, unconsciously following the line of her thoughts, 'what are you going to do about that?'

Tom, about to turn away, stopped and stared at her, his keen country eye apparently noting for the first time her slightly dishevelled appearance. 'I don't rightly follow you, miss,' he replied slowly.

'I think she means the telephone, Tom.' Jason glanced towards her briefly before adding, 'Just go back to the stables, old man, I'll be with you in a minute.

'Go to bed, Miranda,' he ordered, almost before the man had time to turn around. 'There's nothing more you can do tonight.'

Nothing more you can do tonight! Like a parrot Amanda repeated the words silently in her mind. 'Couldn't I come and help?' she offered. 'I'm used to emergencies.'

'Not this sort, my dear.' His eyes mocked intentionally, and suddenly she hated him.

She had been stupid in the drawing-room, and sillier still to imagine that such an interlude with Jason might put their relationship on a friendlier footing. An interlude such as they had shared had been no foundation for anything so comforting as friendship!

'Go to bed, Miranda,' Jason repeated, reaching for his coat, his eyes glinting off her face, reading her thoughts with ironic agreement. 'There's always tomorrow.' The sardonic inflection in his voice made her want to cry.

Growing hot and cold by degrees, Amanda watched him go. In his refusal to accept her help it seemed he had totally rejected her. Could any girl's humiliation be so complete? How could she ever have imagined she might have loved a man like that! She ought to have known that in a few short days such a thing was impossible. Men! On a wave of bitterness she hated the lot of them. Herman, who had made her aware if only indirectly of her body, and now Jason, who must from experience been only too conscious of her half awakened state, and only too ready to supply further tuition.

Rushing upstairs, she flung herself on to her bed for the

74

second time that evening, burying her face in her pillow, feeling the skin burning against the cool linen. She longed desperately for morning, another day, when she would leave Merington for good. Some time during the next evening she would escape, and once at Combe Farm she would be safe for ever. Jason Meade she need never see again!

# CHAPTER FIVE

By late the following afternoon most of the snow had disappeared and Amanda knew it was time for her to go. And when she did go it couldn't have been easier, although her actual journey to Combe Farm was an experience she wouldn't choose to repeat.

She had scarcely seen Jason all day. She had planned to be up early, but exhausted by a surfeit of emotion she had overslept, and it was past breakfast time when she woke to find Mrs Drew standing beside her bed with a tray.

'What time is it?' She'd stared up at Mrs Drew, her eyes wide with dismay.

'Just gone ten, dear. Mr Jason said to let you sleep. They've been out all night with that little horse and she hasn't had her foal yet.' Her eyes wandered curiously to Miranda's pink cheeks, her expression faintly disapproving. 'Mr Jason said you would be tired, but I must say you look all right to me.'

'Of course,' Amanda murmured tersely. 'You shouldn't have bothered bringing me breakfast, anyway.'

'Mr Jason insisted. I've never known him to be like this before.'

Amanda had ignored this, not sure what lay behind Mrs Drew's remark, but annoyed with herself for sleeping in, especially today when she had so much to plan. Perhaps even now the thaw had set in and Jason was waiting to take her into town, to reassure himself about her head? She certainly needed her head examined, but in a different way from what he had in mind!

'Has the vet arrived?' she asked quickly, as Mrs Drew, still frowning suspiciously, turned to go.

'He's been here half the night and he's coming back again this morning.' Inadvertently she told Amanda all she had needed to know.

As soon as the door had closed behind Mrs Drew she had put aside her breakfast tray and scrambled out of bed, rushing to the window to stare out across the garden to the moors beyond. As she had thought, the vet had got here because the snow had all gone. It didn't seem possible, Amanda had blinked, scarcely able to believe her eyes. Just odd patches remained, giving a curious patchwork effect to an otherwise drab landscape. In front of the house the gravel was clear, apart from long pieces of broken grey ice imprinted with tyre marks. It was only on the drive, where the drifting snow had packed hard and deep, that a quantity still lay, but even this had been traversed by the vet's car, as was obvious from the swivelling tracks.

Quickly, after a hasty wash, Amanda dressed and ran downstairs, depositing her tray in the kitchen before running outside. It seemed important to discover if her eyes had been deceiving her from her bedroom window. To her satisfaction it was a morning filled with the promise of a fine day, the wind from the south soft and surprisingly warm after the icy temperatures of late. She went only as far as the garden wall where she turned as if for a final look at the old house, her eyes wandering over the old grey stone, her gaze clinging unconsciously to the deep-set drawing room window where the evening before Jason had almost forced her to respond to him. Useless to recall her own part in that little fiasco. It was only by condemning him completely that she would be able to banish him from her heart.

She hadn't searched for him that morning, much as she had been tempted to. Much as she had longed to go down to the stables she had thought it wiser to stay indoors and help Mrs Drew. In this fashion she hoped to allay any suspicions. She might even convince Jason she hadn't actually noticed the change in the weather, or if she had that she had deliberately decided to ignore it so that she might remain at Merington a little longer.

When Mrs Drew took a basket of sandwiches and tea to the men at four o'clock Amanda stayed behind, grasping the opportunity, after drinking a mug of tea herself, to search for her rucksack in the old brick laundry behind the kitchen. There would be nothing much to put in it, but Jason might think it odd if she left it behind. She had found it almost immediately, and had just been about to pick it up when, to her utter surprise, Jason himself spoke behind her.

He had spoken softly, but her hand which had gone out to pick up the bag had drawn back as if stung. 'I was wondering where you'd got to, Miranda Smith,' he had said.

She had swung around then, totally defensive, praying his sharp eyes hadn't spotted her intentions, saying with some confusion the first thing to enter her head. 'I didn't come down to the stables because I thought you didn't want me any more.'

He had stared at her without answering, and the only sound had been the faint hum from the big deep-freeze behind them, the whisper of the wind beneath the door. It was as if all the taut emotions of the night before had built up to this. A tension between them, almost physical in its reality, too explosive to touch. 'Jason!' she whispered unconsciously.

He had moved in on her then, his glance wholly mocking. 'You do make the silliest remarks.' He had taken a handful of her hair, his hand at her throat, thrusting her back hard against the cold stone wall, his body so near her own she was unable to move. He had bent his head and kissed her full on the mouth. 'Miranda,' he had said, 'I want to apologise for last night. I was in too much of a hurry. This evening will be different, you'll see.'

'No!' said Amanda.

'Yes!' he had replied, with meaningful persistence.

Mrs Drew had returned and Amanda had wrenched herself free with a shudder that went through every inch of her body. There had been no mistaking his intentions! After his horse recovered, he would return to the house, and there would be no resisting him! It was imperative that she get away in good time. She overheard him telling Mrs Drew he should be in before midnight. He might even come to her room. Long before then she must be gone,

78

gone without a trace and on her way to Combe Farm.

It was easier than she had thought possible. Immediately after dinner Mrs Drew said she was going to bed. She had had a headache all day and felt tired.

'I'll wash up,' Amanda said, hurrying her on her way. 'You pop upstairs and when I'm finished I'll bring you a nice cup of tea. Mr Meade and Tom have all they need down at the stables, so you don't need to worry on that score. I think they have enough food to last a week!'

Mrs Drew nodded, needing no persuading, and Amanda swiftly performed the promised tasks, feeling it was the least she could do before she went. Boiling the kettle, she made up a flask and carried it up to Mrs Drew. 'This should last you all night, should you need it,' she smiled.

After that there was nothing left to do but write a short note to Jason which she left in her room. In it she thanked him for allowing her to stay at Merington and explained that she had borrowed three pounds from the petty cash box in the kitchen which she would return as soon as possible. She signed herself simply, Miranda.

The three pounds she actually did take, stuffing them regretfully into her trouser pocket. If the family wasn't back and she couldn't get in or find her shoulder-bag, then she might need some money to see her through until she could get to a bank in the morning. Besides, she thought, with a rather miserable shrug as she let herself out, it would seem more in keeping with the beatnik character she had adopted to take something which did not belong to her. Jason, no doubt, would not be surprised.

A half-moon shone intermittently through the clouds as she left the house. It bathed the wild moors in a surprisingly clear light, but cast long shadows to which Amanda clung, afraid that someone might see her leaving. The drive was still rough with patches of unmelted snow and she tended to stumble, but a peculiar ache in her heart worried her more than her slithering feet, and almost before she reached the end of the drive she was crazily tempted to turn back before anyone discovered her absence.

Thrusting such thoughts to one side, Amanda carried on, walking easily once she was out on to the public road which, to her relief, was clearly signposted. During daylight hours Dartmoor hadn't appeared particularly desolate, but at night a vast opaque gloom seemed to envelop hill and combe alike, at times almost blotting out visibility, giving a rather frightening sense of unreality. As she walked the wind dropped, and the heavy, damp mist which often follows a thaw seemed to creep up around her feet, creating odd distortions, making ordinarily inconspicuous hummocks look like mountains, and the tors to tower in grotesque formations, giving an atmosphere of cruelty and mystery Amanda couldn't shake off. She knew a distinct feeling of mild terror, a feeling that the spirit of the moor was not friendly towards strangers, but rather resentful of those who came from other parts and invaded her fastness. Her blood ran cold as she glanced across the treeless, trackless waste and thought of the pagan rites which might have been enacted here centuries ago, might still be today if the atmosphere of the place was anything to go by.

Jason Meade, she pondered, thinking with a faint shudder of his grim darkness, would surely have ancestors who had practised such black magic. Maybe he still employed a little of that dark propensity himself? Just enough to enable him to capture with surprising ease the emotions of one foolishly impressionable female, should he so desire! If she hurried, she might consider herself fortunate at having escaped so lightly. Wild longings and bitter regrets could be merely a trick, born of the atmosphere of these wild empty spaces. Witchcraft, transilient through space, urging her to return, to surrender herself completely to Jason's arms, was to be ignored as utterly ridiculous! Like a mirage, to which she could be heading, only to find it didn't exist at all, except in her imagination.

A bird flew out of its hiding place where it had settled for the night, startling her, and then she laughed at her own nervous fancies as she came at last to the rambling group of buildings which she took to be Combe Farm. As she turned off the road there was a brief prayer in her heart that she would find Richard and Eva at home. Otherwise she would be sunk! There would be nothing for it but to walk to the nearest village, miles away, and try to find a bed for the night. It would be a long walk, and she would rather not think of the suspicious glances she would be sure to meet at the end of it. Rather than face them, she would as soon sleep here in a barn—only Jason might find her. This time, she thought bitterly, he could add stealing to his former charges of breaking and entering!

It was only when she was actually in the lane leading to the farm that she remembered her bag. To her utter surprise and delight she found it, caught high, yet concealed in a bush which grew out of the side of the gutter. No one would ever have guessed it was there unless they had known where to look, and Amanda's relief in finding it was only surpassed by the fact that the contents appeared to be safely inside, and almost bone-dry. It seemed her luck had changed, decidedly for the better, and hugging her bag to her she was further cheered by the light which she saw, suddenly shining from one of the farmhouse windows. Someone, it seemed, had just switched it on, as it hadn't been there a minute ago. It could surely only be the family?

Heart in her mouth, Amanda ran down the rest of the lane, feeling decidedly foolish, urgently hopeful. No one would ever believe a story such as she had to tell, but then no one must know it! It might be dreadful having to tell a deliberate lie, but better to do that than cause her father and Eva agonies of embarrassment. Besides, the sordid little tale of the last few days might be better not related.

As things turned out she had no need to worry. Richard Trent himself answered the door, and with a faintly surprised grunt bent and kissed her cheek. 'Almost,' he said, 'I didn't recognize you. We only got back ourselves this morning.'

Almost as if she had only been gone since yesterday. Amanda wondered, with a wry grin, if her father, always the most absentminded, recalled exactly how long she had been away.

Eva's greeting was warmer. To Amanda's surprise she found herself folded in a startled but delighted embrace. 'Amanda, my dear, we thought you were on your way back to America!'

'I changed my mind,' Amanda explained.

No one disagreed. They seemed to accept this as quite logical. 'But you've been in London?' Richard asked.

'Yes. My luggage is still at Paddington,' she added quickly, hoping to gloss over this part of the business. With luck no one would ask about times or dates.

'You didn't want to bring it in case we weren't back. It might have been wiser to have rung, but it doesn't matter now that you're here.' Eva smiled cheerfully, inclining her greying head. 'Well, your luggage is no problem, we can send for it right away, but first we'd better go and make up your bed. The heating has been off, but the house is beginning to warm up.'

'Of course,' Richard beamed, still absently, 'it's wonderful to have you.'

'Wonderful,' Eva echoed, and, suddenly with a swift feeling of gratitude Amanda felt like weeping. She hadn't dreamt of a homecoming quite like this. She hadn't anticipated being turned away, but she hadn't thought it possible that two people whom she had seen so little of for years could be so welcoming, especially Eva. Stepmothers, after all, were supposedly unfriendly, but this was surely a fabrication. It was just that she and Eva had never had a chance to know each other properly. Wistfully Amanda thought of time lost, of opportunities that might not come again. Yet it seemed that she and Eva could still be friends, and it never did to dwell too much on that which was past. With an infinitely lighter heart she followed her stepmother upstairs. It was only later, when she was in bed, that she realized no one had so much as mentioned Veronica!

Next morning Eva came to her room and talked. Like Mrs Drew she carried a breakfast tray, and Amanda felt delightfully spoiled. She sighed with sheer pleasure. It was nice, if only this once, to be fussed over as if she was some-one who really mattered. 'At this rate you'll never get rid of me,' she smiled, as Eva placed the tray before her on the bed.

Eva said she was far too thin and looked as if she could stand a little spoiling. And, as she had only just come, who wanted rid of her anyway? 'I think we've left you to your own devices long enough,' she said firmly.

Eva, Amanda decided, was much nicer than she remem-bered. She looked nice, too, with her softly curling hair and grey eyes, her rather matronly figure. She felt oddly surprised that Veronica didn't care for her very much.

'It's good to be here, if only for a little while,' she mur-mured, as Eva, obviously inclined to talk, pulled up a chair and sat down.

'Try to eat everything up, dear,' Eva said mildly, as Amanda drank her coffee but scarcely touched her bacon and eggs. 'You need a bit of flesh on your bones, as I've just told you.'

'I'm sorry, Eva,' Amanda toyed ruefully with her plate of bacon and eggs. 'I don't feel very hungry, and I know good food costs the earth these days.'

Eva shrugged. 'That wasn't the point, darling. Your father's just home from a very successful expedition, so we don't have to consider expense. Not yet . . .'

There was something in the way Eva said it. Amanda glanced at her quickly. 'You mean . . . ?'

A light sigh escaped Eva's lips as she rose and walked to the window. 'I suppose I mean he hasn't changed. Your father is an exceedingly clever biologist, dear, and in the last few weeks has collected enough material to fill several books. He could quite easily make a very good living by doing just that. But no! He'll do his usual tour of lectures, write a few short articles for leading magazines, and I believe there's a TV programme in the offing. Then, after living comfortably for several months, we'll spend whatever's left over on gathering another lot of material in some equally remote corner of the universe.'

Amanda frowned lightly over the rim of her cup. 'Some women would say it was the ideal life. You didn't like Nepal?'

'Of course I liked it, dear. Who wouldn't?' Eva's face lit up momentarily. 'We've been before, as you know, to Central Nepal, but this time we went to Dolpo, one of the drier zones in the west. We had to wait until the monsoons were over in September, then we flew in by light plane, after which we had quite a long trek, but it was wonderful. I suppose I'm still young enough to enjoy that sort of thing, despite the hardships.'

'But old enough to worry about the future, you mean? Richard isn't as young as he used to be.'

A half ashamed smile touched Eva's lips as she noted Amanda's anxious expression. 'I suppose that just about puts it in a nutshell, and it's rather lovely to have one of the family to mention it to, although I'd hate you to imagine it was a major issue.'

'I don't suppose Daddy will ever change.' For as long as Amanda could remember her father had roamed the world. It seemed hardly likely he would stop now. 'Hasn't he anything put away for his old age?' She smiled at Eva ruefully. 'I know he'll never retire, but the day must come when physically he'll be unable to travel.'

'Not a sausage,' Eva replied. 'He doesn't believe in any of the conventional safeguards.'

Amanda grinned, appreciating her stepmother's frankness.

'What about the farm?' she ventured. 'Doesn't this present any security?'

'Not really ...' Eva made a little moue. 'It has possibilities. Richard might be more explicit, but there's only about a hundred acres of rather poor land, not worth a great deal. We rent it out to a farmer at a nominal sum. Of course there's the river, but we've not had much luck with that, so far.'

'The river?' Curiously Amanda waited, but Eva, all of a sudden, appeared to think she had said enough.

84

'Poor Amanda!' she cried. 'Scarcely over the doorstep, and here I am loading you with all my troubles.'

'But I don't mind in the least,' Amanda protested. 'I've always thought this is what real families are for—sharing each other's troubles.'

'Poor child ...' Suddenly compassionate, Eva frowned. 'You don't seem to have had much in the way of family life up till now. After I married your father I must have seemed only too willing to let Veronica take over.'

'That wasn't exactly your fault,' Amanda assured her quickly. 'Veronica thought it would be better for me to live with her. Besides, I was old enough to choose.'

'At sixteen, a very young sixteen, at that, and still at boarding-school! You naturally chose to stay with your sister because she was familiar. I should have tried to arrange things differently instead of taking the easy way out.'

'Never mind,' Amanda smiled, unexpectedly warmed by Eva's honesty. 'I'm here with you now, although I'm not sure how long I can stay. I shall have to get work, or some sort of training. Perhaps you can help me sort something out?'

'Of course,' Eva agreed, while narrowly studying Amanda's too pale face. 'But why not wait a few weeks, spend some time with your father and me? Surely there's no hurry.'

'I seem to have wasted so much time already.' Evasively Amanda searched for an excuse. She couldn't stay here and risk running into Jason Meade. Even to avoid him for a short time might be difficult. Yet she could scarcely explain this to Eva.

Eva was frowning again. 'Didn't you enjoy being in America?'

'The twins were darlings,' Amanda replied quickly, 'and the Randalls were nice. But I wasn't exactly getting anywhere.'

'Young people have so much ambition nowadays ...' There was the noise of a car engine thrusting into the yard below, cutting off whatever else Eva was going to say.

Stopped in mid-sentence, she turned to the window to look out.

'Who is it?' Unconsciously Amanda found herself whispering, fearful that she might well know the answer.

'Someone calling, I expect. I'm just wondering if Richard is around. He went out for a breath of fresh air and I haven't heard him return.' Eva pushed aside the net curtain, and glanced downwards. 'Why, it's Jason Meade!' she spoke after only a slight hesitation of which Amanda was scarcely aware. 'He's our neighbour, in a manner of speaking, although he lives some distance away. He's been keeping an eye on Combe Farm for us, but Richard rang him only this morning to say we were back. We did try last night, before you arrived, but the lines were down or something because we couldn't get through. I'd better pop down and see what he wants. He's not the most patient of men at best of times.'

Irrationally Amanda was almost glad to see her go, fearful that Eva should notice the blood spinning into her face. Her body felt suddenly alive with conflicting emotions, and she sank back against her pillows in an agony of dismay. If she had expected to encounter Jason again, it certainly hadn't been as quickly as this! Her heart pounded and a pulse beat painfully at her temple as she imagined him openly denouncing her to her parents before marching upstairs to drag her out of bed to take his revenge where it really hurt. Eyes glazed with shock, Amanda brushed a trickle of perspiration from her forehead, attempting to steady her shattered nerves. She must try to pull herself together. Jason Meade was a sophisticated man—he wouldn't go to such ridiculous lengths. If he thought of revenge at all it would be in a crueller, more refined fashion, something definitely more subtle than a few well placed wallops with his hand.

With difficulty Amanda controlled a near-sob. This morning she had woken feeling visibly relaxed, well able to cope with any vagaries of her emotions, quite determined to ignore the insidious longings which assailed her heart each time she thought of Jason. Her imagination she had blamed almost exclusively, an equal mixture of weakness and romanticism, precipitated undoubtedly by her recent attack of influenza. In a few ruthless seconds she had been able to dispatch him from her thoughts completely. Yet he had only to appear like this—she didn't actually have to even see him, to make her realize the absolute futility of such resolutions. Jason Meade attracted her in an almost hypnotic fashion, this much she was now forced to admit. She could only pray she wasn't falling in love with him!

Eva's footsteps quickened as she ran downstairs, and there came the sound of a door opening, distant voices. In spite of Amanda's abject fears curiosity prevailed. Impulsively she slid out of bed and silently crept from her room, moving cautiously to the head of the stairs. She seemed to be making a habit of this kind of thing! Combe Farm was much smaller than Merington, having just four up and four down with a straight, wide stair up the middle. Without being seen herself, Amanda was unable to see down below, but she could hear what Eva was saying.

'Do come in, Jason,' she said. 'How nice it is to see you. It's good of you to call so soon.'

'Not at all, Eva . . .' Jason's deep voice carried. 'But I'm afraid this isn't exactly a social call.'

Then, to Amanda's utter chagrin, Eva said quickly, almost as if she suspected someone listening and was afraid that Jason's missive might be confidential, 'Won't you join me for coffee, Jason? I have it ready in the kitchen.'

Jason must have nodded his assent as Amanda didn't hear any more, just the sound of their footsteps receding, the murmur of Eva's low voice as the kitchen door closed. On a tremulously drawn breath Amanda went back to her room, her eyes dark with a hint of strain.

Not long afterwards she heard Jason go. From behind the concealing lace curtains her view was unimpaired. Down there, standing beside his car, he wasn't so many yards away, and she stared bleakly at the top of his dark head as he bent to hear something Eva was saying. When he looked up she could almost see the tired lines on his face, the grim set of his firmly shaped mouth, and she wondered, inadvertently, if the little mare had safely had her foal. She would hate to think anything had gone seriously wrong, yet what else could account for Jason's forbidding expression? Certainly not her own disappearance. Most likely he had forgotten all about her, in spite of her brief fears to the contrary.

'Richard hasn't turned up yet, but Jason wouldn't wait. Scarcely stopped long enough to have his coffee,' Eva said, when Amanda came downstairs a little later. 'He just called to see if we'd noticed anyone around. It seems there've been a few suspicious strangers lately.'

'Really!'

'Umm . . .' Eva had already forgotten. 'I told him there was no one here but the three of us. He knows Richard has a young daughter, and I told him you'd come from Town with us. It saved going into details. Besides, he was in a hurry.'

A little later, when the washing-up was completed, she glanced at Amanda rather quickly and said, 'I think I'd better mention, darling, before your father returns, that we've had a letter from Veronica. It was with the rest of our mail yesterday when we collected it from the post office.'

Amanda's heart beat apprehensively. Veronica had threatened, but she hadn't taken her very seriously. Yet whatever she had written couldn't have been so very incriminating. Eva didn't look particularly put out.

'She said,' Eva went on, 'that you'd had some silly misunderstanding, and you had disappeared. She had hoped to find you, but you seemed to have vanished without a trace. Your old nannie had heard from you, so she was sure you must be all right, but she and Herman had searched in vain.'

Amanda's face went white. 'Was this all she said?'

'Not exactly, dear.' Eva frowned doubtfully. 'There were, I must admit, a few disparaging remarks about your morals, that you'd tried to lead poor Herman astray. Richard doesn't care for Herman, I'm afraid, so he just laughed at that one. He promptly put the letter in the fire and merely said you'd probably only learnt the gentle art of self-defence. We all know Veronica could never tolerate opposition of any kind.'

Clearly there wasn't much sympathy between Eva and Veronica, but Richard and Veronica had always been good friends. Amanda murmured unhappily, glancing away from Eva's slightly curious face, 'I hope my quarrel with Veronica didn't upset Daddy too badly?'

Eva made a wry grimace. 'Veronica and your father weren't very amicably disposed last time they saw each other,' she confessed, 'but that had nothing to do with you.'

'No?'

'No . . .' Eva hesitated, 'it had to do with the river.'

'The river?'

'In a way . . .' Again there was a slight hesitation. 'You see, dear, we have almost a mile of rather valuable salmon fishing on the river. Some of the best fishing in Devon, I believe, and it runs through the middle of our land. Well, Jason Meade, who was here this morning, whom you have yet to meet, would like it. He would like it because he has a hotel which adjoins our land, and it would be an invaluable addition to his business.'

There was an odd little silence. Jason Meade, Amanda thought desperately—was she never to escape him completely? That he was involved with the family here at Combe Farm was becoming obvious. His involvement with Veronica she already knew about, if in a roundabout way, but that it could be because of a river seemed highly improbable. It was a surprise, too, to learn he had a hotel so near! Alarming as well as surprising, making Amanda realize how difficult it might be to avoid him. She said, 'I don't see what the river has to do with Veronica.'

Eva smiled ruefully, unaware of Amanda's unhappiness. 'Well, if Richard were to get a good price for the land, including the river, we could put it aside as a sort of nest-egg. Remember we talked of it earlier? We aren't in any great hurry, but this is why Richard is holding out for a good price, and he thought Jason might give him one. Veronica, you see, had almost promised he would.'

'How could she do that?' Cold suspicion clutched Amanda's heart, even before Eva enlightened her.

'We were sure that Jason was in love with Veronica and intended marriage. At weekends, when Veronica came down from London and Jason was at Merington, they saw a lot of each other. Jason Meade is a wealthy man, my dear, as well as a very attractive one. Can you wonder he's so popular with the opposite sex? But there's no reason to suppose he won't settle down one day and marry. We had hoped it would be with Veronica, but it seems we were mistaken.'

Later, while she explored down by the river, Amanda grimly considered what Eva had told her. Not until now, when she was on her own, had she even dared to think about it. Had Veronica really been in love with Jason, or he with her? She hardly supposed it likely that Jason Meade would stop at nothing to get his hands on a mile of fishing, but undoubtedly it would be an asset, and he might have been encouraging Veronica with this in mind. On the other hand, he might have been genuinely in love with her and turned bitter when she rejected him for another man.

If Richard had hoped to procure a more than agreeable price from Jason, a price which would provide the security Eva craved, and also leave a roof over their heads as Jason would have little use for the house at Combe Farm, then he too might be feeling bitter. But was Richard being absolutely fair in blaming Veronica? Veronica might have her faults, but it seemed to Amanda that she had been dangled like a bait on the end of a hook. First by Richard in order to get more money for his land, and then by Jason in a despicable attempt to purchase what he wanted cheaply. Only one thing puzzled Amanda greatly. How had her sister, after knowing a man like Jason Meade, escaped wholehearted enough to marry someone else?

Over lunch Eva said to Richard, 'Jason called. He seemed a bit unsettled about something—I can't remember exactly. I believe he did ask if we'd seen any suspicious characters around. Anyway, he wants us to go over for a drink one evening, Amanda too. I said we'd better wait a few days until we were settled in, and he promised to ring nearer the weekend.'

Amanda's heart sank as she heard Richard agree. If she had thought vaguely that any social contact between Combe Farm and Merington might have ended with Veronica's marriage then she had been mistaken. On the surface at least there was still apparently some pretence of friendship. Perhaps both Richard and Jason still hoped to achieve their goal, if in other ways.

One thing Amanda was sure about. She wouldn't herself be attending any cocktail party at Merington. She would have to think of some excuse. This time it might not be so difficult, but if there were to be continuous comings and goings then the whole situation would be impossible. She would either have to return to London, or, failing this, to see Jason personally and confess. It should be relatively easy to explain, to make light of the whole matter. Surely the latter would be the more sensible thing to do? Yet, as before, she shrank from his anger, and the possibility that he might choose to inflict some form of revenge which she would rather not contemplate. How could she when she remembered the force of her feelings for him, the quivering awareness she had felt in his arms? A shiver went through her, an agony of sensitive nerves, leaving her as completely indecisive as before.

The end of the week came and went with Richard and Eva spending an enjoyable Saturday evening at Merington. Amanda stayed unhappily at home. It had been, Eva told her, quite a party!

'One could scarcely believe it,' she laughed, buttering Sunday morning toast. 'They've had quite a storm. After all the fine weather this week it doesn't seem possible, but Jason was telling us he's been snowed up for days!'

'Does he live there by himself?' Amanda heard herself asking, not because she didn't know the answer, but rather because of a sudden urgent desire to go on talking about him. If she couldn't see him it was, in some small measure, a solace to her aching heart to hear what he was doing.

'All by himself,' Eva confirmed brightly. 'He does have a Mrs Drew who lives with her husband in a cottage, and comes in when Jason is entertaining. But otherwise he appears to enjoy being on his own. I suppose it does make a change from his usual routine as during summer he's amongst people all the time.'

'He might get married?' Why couldn't she leave it alone?

Eva smiled. 'I don't know if I'd enjoy being married to a man like that. He would want all his own way.'

It wasn't until the following week that Amanda received her first big fright. Eva asked if she would drive Richard into Newton Abbot where he had some rather urgent business to see to. Eva was too busy to go herself.

'I know he drives, darling,' she retorted, when Amanda pointed this out, 'but his eyesight isn't as good as it used to be—or he's just getting more absent-minded, I'm not sure which. Anyway, I would feel happier if you would go with him. I have this talk about Nepalese women to give to the local W.I. this evening, and I don't seem to have it even half prepared.'

Amanda's luggage had arrived and had all been unpacked and put away in the huge old oak wardrobe in her room, but mistakenly she had decided to wear her old denim slacks, thinking they would be more comfortable to drive in than a skirt. Her mood brighter, she drove her father without mishap to Newton Abbot. She hadn't realised how good it was to be out and about again. For almost two weeks she had hardly dared to leave the immediate vicinity of the farm for fear of meeting Jason. Now she felt like a fly released from a web of its own making, lighthearted enough to laugh a little at her own foolish fancies. Time, she supposed, had a way of blunting the edge of even the worst fears.

On the way the moors swept before her, drab in November, but with rivers and tors, wide distances to explore. And she had wasted time hiding from a man who had probably never given her another thought.

And if these conclusions brought only a negative comfort,

at least they released some of Amanda's frozen vitality, which enabled her to park the car and say goodbye to Richard on a new wave of optimism. She arranged to meet him later, after he had completed his business.

Afterwards she wandered, touring the shops, exploring a little, Devon Square and the town's Italian-style Courtenay Park, but it grew too cold and dull to see very much. It was then, in the gathering dusk as she went in search of a newsagent to buy Eva a magazine, that she saw him. He came driving down the street as she waited to cross. He was driving a beautiful blue Mercedes coupé which drew her eyes automatically. And, just as she stared at it, he turned his head, meeting her eyes in a blinding flash of recognition!

Just for one split second, as she stood unable to move, as the blood pounded untrammelled through her body, did she stare at him. Then the big car moved with the heavy flow of evening traffic, and he was gone.

# CHAPTER SIX

As they drove from the multi-storey car park Richard Trent glanced reflectively at his daughter's white face, and there was unusual concern in his voice as he said, 'I wish you'd let me get you a drink before we left. I can't think what Eva will say.'

Trying to keep her own voice on an even keel, Amanda replied, 'Stop worrying, Daddy. I had some tea in a small café about three, and as you've had something yourself there doesn't seem to be much point in drowning ourselves in more.'

Richard sighed, frowning at his briefcase before he turned to thrust it suddenly on to the back seat. 'I have two daughters,' he mused heavily, 'and I'm not sure that I understand either of them.'

'Well, there's still time!' Unable, in spite of herself, to restrain a slight smile, Amanda replied lightly. The slightly exaggerated pathos in her father's tones had not escaped her. She could have pointed out that owing to his penchant for foreign parts he had rarely given himself a chance to understand anything. His family had usually been relegated to second place, and any responsibility he might have felt had usually been thrust on to other people. Was it surprising if he was beginning to realize this for himself?

He pondered, still frowning. 'It would seem I've been guilty of neglect, although it didn't occur to me at the time. Perhaps your American trip was a mistake—Veronica appears to think so.'

'It was Veronica's idea to begin with.'

'Yes, and while I didn't know Bill Randall personally, I knew of his reputation. He and his wife are a brilliant team. I thought you could do worse. And when I spoke to him on the telephone, he did promise to keep an eye on you.'

'Which he did,' Amanda retorted flatly, her eyes stoically

on the road ahead. 'You mustn't take what Veronica told you regarding that too seriously. The Randalls scarcely let me out of their sight, which occasionally grew irksome.'

'You were with them almost two years . . .'

Doubt edged her father's tones and Amanda's lips tightened impatiently. 'If you remember, most of the time we lived in the Everglades—a luxurious cabin, I'll admit, but in a very isolated position. Apart from the rest of the research outfit, who were mostly married couples, I often saw no one else for weeks on end. And it was Veronica's idea that I stayed on.'

Richard stirred uncomfortably, as if his conscience suddenly troubled him. 'I'm afraid I've always let Veronica have too much of her own way, especially where you've been concerned, and she repays me by marrying the wrong man!'

Amanda's smile flickered again, this time with genuine amusement. She need not have worried that Richard would concentrate long on her troubles when he obviously imagined he had plenty of his own. The slightly self-centred set of his face pronounced it. Veronica's marriage had clearly disappointed him, but probably only because it had interfered with his immediate plans. There was only an unexplainable relief in her own heart that Veronica hadn't married Jason Meade. 'Veronica appears to be in love with Herman,' she pointed out, after a small pause.

'Yes, yes . . .' Richard's mood changed testily. 'Herman's all right, I suppose. But that doesn't alter the fact that she married him without a thought for her parents. She could have managed things better, I'm convinced.'

Much of this Amanda couldn't fathom out. 'Because of the river, I suppose?'

Richard sniffed self-righteously. 'I perceive you and Eva have been talking?'

Amanda sighed. She had promised Eva she wouldn't say anything about knowing, but it had just slipped out. 'Eva only said you hoped to sell the fishing. I don't think she intended betraying any secrets. It was probably only because Mr Meade called that she mentioned it at all.'

Richard said, 'The point is they were friendly, and I think she could have exerted some influence. She knew it was important. She could at least have waited until we had a favourable decision.'

Amanda changed gear on a steep hill, driving on silently, her thoughts preoccupied. For as long as she could remember Richard had always been childishly indignant when people chose not to think his way, but if he was disappointed in Veronica what would he say if he was to learn of her own unfortunate adventures with Jason Meade? He would consider—and rightly—that so far as the river was concerned, his younger daughter had probably finished off his chances of selling it completely. Viewed from this angle it seemed more imperative than ever that Jason shouldn't discover her true identity. And absolutely essential that she returned to London as soon as possible.

Feeling Richard's impatient eyes on her face, she suggested soothingly and with more composure than she felt, 'If the river would prove a marvellous asset to Mr Meade I shouldn't have thought he'd let anyone or anything stand in his way. If, as you say, he was annoyed when Veronica married someone else, well, this is understandable, but I'm sure he's not a man to mix business with pleasure.'

'You haven't by any chance met him?' Of a sudden Richard looked suspicious, noting the faint flush of colour on Amanda's cheeks.

'No, of course not,' she gulped, her voice shaking, praying he wouldn't notice. Sometimes he could be surprisingly astute. It was dreadful having to hide the truth, but worse still to be forced to tell deliberate lies. A wave of remorse hit her, almost physical in its impact, making her feel slightly sick. Why was it that everything appeared much worse than it had done this morning? Seeing Jason in Newton Abbot seemed the culmination of two weeks of misery, affecting her more than she dared to admit. Rather desperately she tried to shut out the image of his dark face, to concentrate on the more practical aspects. There was relief in the knowledge she had posted the three pounds which she had owed him. Even if he hadn't seen her he would have known she was still in Devon from the postmark on the envelope, so it was little use pretending to be alarmed on that account. Her unhappiness stemmed from the vivid reactions which she had felt flood through her as she had watched him drive past. The vivid flash of anger, flicking her momentarily from eyes diamond-hard beneath dark brows, was with her yet, and it was with some effort that she dragged her thoughts away and began talking with her father of other things.

Driving home that evening she had planned to return to London within the next few days, but try as she might, she could not bring herself to suggest it. Although they didn't actually put it into words, there emanated from Richard and Eva the distinct impression that she was needed, and, rather than hurt them, she hid her own uncertainty and stayed on. Time, at Combe Farm, she found, swirled by like the Sea of Tranquillity, the short, dark days making the evenings cosy, rendering a certain languor to the spirit, a drugged dullness to overcome any instinctive urge to escape. Valuable time was lost when even the thought of a career was something to be put to one side until tomorrow. Eva, furiously preparing Christmas cakes and puddings, refused almost point blank to allow Amanda to do anything constructive.

'I refuse to be done out of a real family Christmas,' she declared. 'Something will turn up in the New Year, you'll see.'

Amanda nodded, faintly troubled but not unwilling to be persuaded as she whisked eggs and creamed butter, following carefully Eva's instructions. The farmhouse kitchen, though not so big as Jason's, was warm and comfortable, more homely with a kettle singing on the old coal range and a cat with two kittens purring beside it. There was also Sam, Eva's small Jack Russell terrier, who had been boarded out while they'd been away. Now, king of the castle once more, he sat nodding approvingly, like a little old man, yapping at every small noise he heard but adding immeasurably to the domestic scene. While Eva was abroad he had been left with

97

one of her friends who lived a few miles away. This same friend, she said, was giving a small dance and barbecue during the following week, in aid of charity, and she had bought three tickets.

'She gives it every year,' she explained, not noticing Amanda's despairing face, 'and usually there are a lot of young people. It would be nice for you to meet someone of your own age. You might even find someone special. You're a very attractive girl, darling, suppose I do say it myself.'

'There seems little point in knowing people if eventually I'm to work in London,' Amanda replied evasively.

'Nonsense,' Eva retorted briskly, picking up a cup of coffee for Richard. 'Even if you did, there are always week-ends. I don't intend losing sight of you again.'

Not even a little comforted, Amanda worked hard throughout the remainder of the day. It was only by working like a Trojan and keeping herself occupied that she was able to keep her unhappy thoughts at bay. Later that evening when Veronica rang from Washington her mood was such that she didn't really care what her sister might say.

Eva, as usual, answered the call. Richard had no great respect for telephones and liked to pretend they weren't there. 'That was Veronica,' she told them, a few minutes later. 'I'm afraid she's still worrying about you, Amanda, but I was able to put her mind at rest.'

'You told her I was here?' Amanda glanced quickly towards her father, who, apart from an indifferent nod, had subsided behind his newspaper again.

Eva said of course she had told Veronica she was here, and enjoying herself enormously. And quite the belle of the neighbourhood! 'Well, you could be, my dear,' she added brightly, 'if you would bother to circulate a bit.'

'What had Veronica to say about that?' Amanda asked on a surge of dismay. What on earth had possessed Eva to say such a thing? She must know Veronica got jealous! And, even from America, Veronica's jealousy could have reper-cussions.

'Ha,' said Eva, quite unrepentant, and oblivious, too, of

Amanda's consternation. 'I'm afraid she didn't seem to like it one bit!'

Afterwards, Amanda tried to convince herself she was letting a ridiculous imagination have too much of its own way. There was absolutely nothing Veronica could do. In her own mind Amanda had previously gone over all the possibilities and found them negative. It was possible that Veronica might try again to blacken her character, especially now she knew she was here, but she had little to go on, and Amanda doubted if either Richard or Eva would so much as listen. That her renewed doubts were in any way wrapped up with Jason Meade she refused to consider. She didn't intend seeing him again, so it mattered not one jot whether he knew about Herman and the bathroom or not. Such a tale was unlikely to interest him in any case, even if he should ever come to realize who she was. And Amanda was determined he should not!

All three Trents had been invited to the party the next week and, as Eva kept the tickets displayed on the mantelpiece in the sitting-room, it was impossible to forget. This time Amanda couldn't bring herself to produce her usual excuse, and in the end she said frankly, if rather shamefacedly, that she would rather not go. Richard, as usual not greatly interested, only shrugged, but Eva was cross. 'You'll never make friends at this rate,' she protested. 'You should try to be sociable. Besides, what are people to think?'

Remorse pricked Amanda severely as she watched them depart, and impulsively she almost changed her mind about staying at home. But it was a temptation which couldn't be contemplated, much as she felt like a change of scene. An evening spent entirely alone with her own turbulent thoughts might be anything but inviting, yet what other choice did she really have? To run the risk of meeting Jason Meade was sheer foolishness, especially now that Richard's river supplied a further complication. Richard had said only that morning that he had seen Jason, and Jason was still thinking of buying. Her own personal problems might not matter so much once that was settled. The thing she hated most was having to hurt Eva without being able to explain the reason why.

After they had gone she had a bath, then drying herself quickly, she put on her jeans again, not bothering to change into a dress. There didn't seem much point when she was on her own and, when the moon was brighter, she might take the dog along the lane for his evening walk.

In the sitting-room she turned down the lights and switched on the TV. There wasn't anything she really wanted to watch, but it might prove a distraction if nothing else. She didn't feel hungry enough to eat any supper and it was too early to go out with Sam. In fact the programme she chose proved diverting—a period play set in Cornwall, in the last century, and the male lead was played by a man in his late thirties, a man who looked very much like Jason Meade. Dark, he was, with the same hint of ruthlessness about his mouth, the same impression of latent strength, of temper held finely in check, controlling but not entirely subduing a smouldering suggestion of passion.

Amanda shuddered as he swept the girl he desired into his arms, kissing her rebellious lips with deliberate intent, his arms restraining her struggling body with practised ease. So absorbed was she that she failed to hear the car draw up outside. Nor was she aware of a door slamming, and someone walking towards the house, until Sam started barking. Even then, with her senses pleasantly relaxed, she found nothing alarming in the knock which sounded through the house as the heavy old door-knocker rose and fell, as the silence which followed announced clearly someone waited for an answer.

It didn't occur to Amanda to ponder deeply on who might be there. Though sensitive to a degree, she wasn't by nature particularly nervous or frightened at being left on her own. Old houses, for her, held no terror, she had always found them comforting. With a quiet word to Sam she switched off the TV. It was possibly a neighbour with a message, or calling casually to borrow something, not an entirely unheard-of occurrence even at this time of night. Firmly she drew back the old-fashioned bolt which Eva always told her to use if she was in alone, and opened the door with an inquiring smile—a smile which froze on her lips when she saw who it was who stood there on the step. None other but Jason Meade!

Almost daily Amanda had expected something like this to happen, but until now fate had been kind, protecting her, it had seemed, from such a disaster. Now it appeared her luck had run out, as, nerves stretched to breaking point, she stared at him with wide, frightened eyes, wondering if she was seeing aright. In that instant the hall seemed suddenly to be swirling around her, blurring and dissolving as she was swept away in the ice-cold displeasure of his eyes, greeny-grey eyes, cold like wintry seas which threatened to drown her, and defensively she flung a hand across her face, hoping that when she looked again he would be gone.

But unfortunately he proved no figment of her imagination. Another glance convinced her, but as she gazed into the dark face of the man who so strangely haunted her dreams, a sense of unreality overtook her. How had she ever hoped to escape him? Shock, eclipsing anything she had known before, paralysed her tongue, washing the hot colour from her cheeks and leaving her creamy pale, visibly shaken. She drew a quick, shuddery breath, audible in the charged atmosphere.

Jason spoke first, after that steady, calculating appraisal, and, even knowing he was angry, she was in no way prepared for the harsh coldness of his voice. 'Why the hell didn't you tell me!' The question hit her, full of a leashed violence, giving her no quarter.

Taut with a saving indignation, Amanda suddenly found her own voice and answered back, 'You never gave me a chance.'

'A chance? Good God!' His white teeth snapped together, as his hands went out, clamping like steel on her shoulders. 'How else would you describe almost a week spent in my company? You had each day, hours, when only a few minutes would have sufficed—and you say you had no chance!'

'I still say it ...' Her voice choked, caught in the pulse beating heavily at the base of her throat, burnt in the flame which spread where his hands curved the fine bone against her neck. Never had she seen him like this, eyes dark and flashing, furrows of emphasis and tension between his dark brows.

He caught and held her eyes with the hard, cynical look in his. 'Let's go inside,' he said tersely, almost thrusting her back as he slammed the door. 'If nothing else you owe me some sort of explanation.'

Almost as if he owned the house he propelled her in front of him into the sitting-room, his hands leaving her shoulders to fasten with continuing relentlessness on the soft flesh of her upper arms, eliminating any possibility of escape. In front of the fire he stopped and released her abruptly, as if the touch of her tried even his inexhaustible control. 'Now you can begin to talk,' he said smoothly. 'And we'll have the truth for a change.'

Amanda couldn't think straight. Her mind still whirled in dazed little circles. 'How did you know I was here?' she gasped. 'Or did you just call to see Daddy and Eva?'

His narrowed eyes moved over her lovely flushed face, and he laughed sarcastically. 'A woman's curiosity must always be satisfied! But it might be a pleasure to tell you so much—just enough to illustrate that deception doesn't really pay.'

'I didn't deliberately set out to deceive anyone,' she protested.

'Just shut up for a minute, won't you!' He advanced again and she retreated, stumbling back into a chair, from where she continued to stare at him. He towered above her, a hard mocking light flaring in his eyes at her physical helplessness. 'Right at this moment,' he said, 'I'd like to break you in two, but that might not serve any useful purpose. You want to know how I discovered your whereabouts? This evening when your parents arrived at Newton Hall without you, it suddenly struck me that there was something very peculiar about a girl who always stayed at home. You might call it intuition, but I suddenly realized that Richard's mysterious young daughter was none other but you.'

'Intuition?' Amanda repeated, shivering in spite of herself. This man was surely half devil, as she had suspected when she had left his house on the moors.

'Don't look at me like that,' he rasped, eyes glittering. 'I've always found it extremely useful.'

'Not regarding me, surely!' she challenged.

'But yes,' he replied, with soft irony which was wholly deceptive. 'I talked, I'll admit deliberately, to Eva. She was hurt and rather puzzled at not being able to persuade you to come out. And while she talked I thought of other occasions. The time when I called at Combe Farm the morning after you'd disappeared. The evening I asked you all around for drinks and only Richard and Eva turned up. Then, a few minutes after seeing you in Newton Abbot, I happened also to spot Richard. Suddenly this evening at Newton everything seemed to fall into place. I was, shall we say, convinced that I knew exactly where to find Miranda Smith. And as you see I wasn't mistaken.'

His eyes held hers, moving across her face coolly, but his voice bit into her like a whiplash. Amanda made a desperate bid to emulate that coolness. 'So,' she said, 'you left the party and barged straight in here. You didn't wonder if you'd be welcome!'

'You misjudge me, my dear,' his voice was silky. 'I'm not totally a barbarian. I had to return for a short while to Merington, and merely suggested to Eva that I called here on my way back, that I might, by using a little gentle persuasion, induce you to change your mind and return with me to the ball.'

'That was despicable! Of course I shan't come.'

'But I think you will, Miranda ...' His tones held a suave threat, his continuing use of her fictitious name indicating that he was not yet prepared to overlook that which was past. 'The night is still young,' he went on. 'Time enough for you to change your mind. But first you're going to tell me why you didn't tell me who you were in the first place, and why you walked out on me without a word of thanks?'

'I left a note!' Already she had decided not to go with him one yard, and a fine defiance flared in her eyes as she stared up at him from the comparative safety of her chair. In an evening jacket with a white, ruffled shirt, he looked incredibly handsome, but also devastatingly hard. Not a man to be distracted from a chosen course, or turned by feminine wiles into something less than he was. The few words she murmured could hardly have made less impression.

He repeated now, with enticing sharpness, 'You left a note—and Mrs Drew found it.'

'I left it on my dressing-table.'

'And how did you expect me to find it on your dressing-table?'

Colour flooded Amanda's face vividly as she became aware of the trap he had set so deviously. Jason knew what she had thought he had in mind that evening and was punishing her accordingly. When she didn't reply, but sat in sullen silence, he reached down, jerking her to her feet with a ruthless gesture, his fingers hurting again on her arm.

'You thought I intended coming to your room,' he said.

'No ...' Her flush deepened, both mentally and physically. His hands hurt, yet filled her with a riotous fire, and she squirmed. 'That is—I don't know,' she gasped, illogically breathless. 'You thought I was just wandering around, looking for amusement. A man doesn't always respect a girl like that.'

'Miranda,' he rapped, his eyes travelling over her narrowly, 'it could quite easily have happened, but I assure you I had no intention of going to your room that night, but such an incident might serve to illustrate the absolute folly of your actions. Another man might not have resisted such a temptation. Why in heaven's name didn't you tell me who you were to start with? You could have saved yourself much embarrassment. Didn't you realize you were playing a dangerous game?'

Amanda's breath hurt sharply, and her thick lashes flickered. There was some look on his dark face, some indefinite change in him which supplied the missing text to what he said. He wasn't, she thought, a man given to platitudes. Why hadn't he told her outright exactly what he had in mind? He didn't even have to spell it out—she understood only too well! When he had kissed her, held her in his arms, he had only been amusing himself. He had accepted her at face value, and was now making it quite clear that otherwise he wouldn't have touched her. His involvement had been purely of the senses. No serious interpretation must be put on what had been only a little lighthearted dalliance. How strange that such an impression hurt!

Rather desperately her mind spun back to the beginning, as the green flame behind his smouldering glance warned her his patience stretched thinly. 'If you'd waited before tipping me off that ladder,' she countered, 'you might have been saved a lot of embarrassment yourself.'

'Don't be damned silly!' The dark, devastating voice stung and his lean fingers tightened. 'You did come around. At any rate in the house you could have confessed, the effort wouldn't have strained you. What were you doing, anyway, creeping in here like an escaped convict from the prison?'

'I wasn't . . .' Amanda's small white teeth clamped tight.

'Oh, yes, you were! Don't contradict me, Miss Miranda-Amanda! There was some particular reason, and on top of this, another reason why you didn't tell me. I haven't got it quite worked out, but don't worry, it will come!'

He was hateful, completely despicable, and his guess was too near for comfort. She retorted quickly, 'I was ill, if you remember! Was it surprising I couldn't think straight?'

'You'd better think again, Amanda,' he said dryly.

'Perhaps I liked your house, Mr Meade. Combe Farm, with the electricity cut off, didn't sound inviting.' Head flung back, she stared at him defiantly.

He wasn't impressed. 'But you aren't that sort of a girl —or so you tell me. Obviously your parents don't know you spent a few offbeat days with me. One wonders what they would think should I tell them?'

'You wouldn't dare!'

'Never dare a fool, Miss Smith!'

Amanda gulped, her face hot, breath coming too quickly. 'I don't know what you're getting at,' she said nervously.

'You could be teasing me?'

'Not a hope,' he drawled, his eyes on her flushed cheeks. 'So what do we do with Miranda Smith? Bury her decently, or would you rather have a public announcement?'

'No, not that!' She turned away from him, jerking her shoulder from his hands as a thrill of fear went through. How she wished she might shatter his enormous self-esteem by laughing in his face, but she dared not. One day, perhaps, if she had patience! She swallowed hard. 'I would be grateful if you didn't mention anything to anyone. Not for my own sake,' she assured him, 'but because of Richard and Eva.'

'Naturally,' he nodded, the quirk at the side of his mouth sarcastic. 'One must consider them.'

Amanda ignored this, as another thought descended terrifyingly. 'What about the Drews?' she gasped. 'Have you forgotten?'

'You can safely leave the Drews to me,' he replied. 'They've been with me for years and have every comfort, something they're not liable to jeopardize in a hurry. Besides, I think they liked you.'

'Thank you,' Amanda whispered tonelessly.

He laughed, without mirth. 'Don't be in too much of a hurry to thank me, Amanda. I'm not in the habit of doing something for nothing.'

Incensed at that, she flung around at him furiously.

'You intend using blackmail!'

He grinned at that, but entirely wickedly, 'Nothing so dramatic, Amanda, although if you care to put it that way,

106

yes. I was merely about to suggest you made a little more effort to be pleasant.'

'Which might be difficult,' she retorted rashly, 'where you're concerned. You haven't exactly put yourself out to be nice to me.'

'Haven't I, Amanda?' his eyes glinted. 'Your memory isn't nearly as good as my own. However,' as colour vividly tinted her skin, 'a fresh start might be good for both of us.'

Refusing to admit even this much, Amanda asked sullenly, and with a hint of apprehension, 'What do you actually want me to do?'

The glint in his eyes deepened with punishing intentness. 'That, Amanda, would take too long to explain. To begin with you can go and put on something more suitable for the party—to which I will escort you.'

Amanda felt struck, somewhere where it hurt most. Events were moving too rapidly, she needed a breathing space in which to marshal her chaotic thoughts, not to be hauled out immediately like some erring adolescent refusing to go to school. Why should she agree to the demands of this man who stood before her? Would not she be only sinking deeper into a mire of deception by agreeing to do as he wished? Yet, in her heart, she knew for the moment she had no defence. Any defensive tactics she chose to employ must be considered later, when she was in a different frame of mind. Not now, when because of Jason's dominating presence she wasn't able to even think clearly. At the moment it was all beyond her comprehension. He didn't even like her, yet he insisted she went with him to Newton Hall!

Uncertainly she stared up at him. 'Surely, if I turn up with you this evening, Daddy and Eva will wonder?'

'Nonsense,' his tones brooked no further argument, 'didn't I tell them I would collect you!'

Just like that, Amanda thought angrily, as she ran upstairs and began searching through her wardrobe for something suitable! Perhaps she ought to have asked what he had in mind? He was the sort of man, she suspected, who liked a woman to look smart. His awareness of beauty was something she felt in her bones. Whatever else a girl might have, she would be of little use to him unless she had also a certain attractiveness. Amanda quivered, an uncontrollable reaction as she flung herself into the task of choosing a dress, attempting, with a dismal lack of success, to banish him from her thoughts.

Why should he want more of her company anyway? Hadn't he been brutally frank with her at Merington? She had attracted him in a certain way, but one way only! So why was he bothering now? Perhaps, in spite of his threats, he would soon lose interest. Perhaps after this one evening? As it was he obviously considered she had made a fool of him by not telling him who she was, and was not prepared to overlook it immediately.

Amanda frowned as she removed a dress from its hanger. She supposed it was, in a way, her own fault that she found herself in her present position. She should have told him, and if she hadn't overheard him talking to Veronica on the telephone she might have done. Yet then she might never have known those days at Merington—that evening in his arms! Swiftly she clamped down on such thoughts and made a determined effort this time, forcing herself to remove the protective wrapper from a white chiffon dress, to shake out the cloudy folds of it. There was another—For a hesitant moment her eyes lingered on a silky blue nylon jersey which she had bought in London and never yet worn. Reluctantly she left it where it was. It was special, not for this evening, she decided firmly, closing the wardrobe door.

As she had already bathed it was a simple matter to discard her slacks and slip into her dress. It was the small things she lingered over. Suddenly it seemed important that she looked nice. The white chiffon was conventional with its low round neckline and long full sleeves, but the skirt swirled about her ankles in a very feminine way when she walked. And a little carefully applied make-up, she decided, would make all the difference. A few minutes later, well satisfied, she brushed out her hair, liking the way it fluffed out on to her shoulders. It was growing quickly, framing her face gently from its centre parting, and full of gleaming lights. Her reflection in the mirror told her she looked attractive, and because of this she felt a little confidence returning, so that she was able to glance at Jason with a cool little nod as she ran downstairs again.

'I'm ready,' she stated, lifting her chin and swinging her short creamy fur wrap.

He nodded and came slowly towards her, his eyes appreciative on her slender, curved figure. He said with a slight smile, his glance lingering, 'Do you realize this is the first time I've seen you in a dress?'

Determined he shouldn't suspect the uneven beating of her heart, she dropped in a slightly exaggerated curtsey. 'I hope you approve of what you see, Mr Meade,' she replied coldly.

'Jason,' he instructed, 'from now on. You'd do well to remember.'

On the way to Newton Hall there were things she intended to ask him, but she suddenly found she could not. He wasn't, she was discovering, a man easily approachable, and although she had decided to ask him frankly about his relationship with Veronica, the query stayed on the tip of her tongue and got no further. Nor did she dare mention her flight from Merington, in spite of an urgent desire to know exactly when he had discovered her missing, and she silently berated herself for not thinking of it sooner. She ought to have asked earlier, when he had first arrived that evening. She ought to have kept her own wits about her instead of being thrown into such a state of confusion that all the important issues had flown from her head. As she sat beside him every nerve in her body cried out to know how he had felt after she had gone. Yet despairingly she knew he would never tell her, not now. The impulsiveness of the moment when he might have done had gone.

For a long time, it seemed, she sat beside him not

speaking, attempting to ignore him, fighting her own personal involvement but incurably defeated by her uncontrollable emotions. There was, she supposed, a certain humour in the situation, but it didn't quite reach her. She had sought to deceive him, and he had turned the tables neatly, obviously enjoying his revenge. He had satisfied her curiosity only so far. He had told her of his fury at her headlong flight from his house, but he would never admit to any heartache. That would be entirely out of character, as well as being untrue. The sort of confession she longed to hear would never pass his lips, and she was only deluding herself ever to think it would.

At last, with a hint of desperation, she asked, 'Did the foal arrive safely?'

'Eventually . . .'

She glanced at his clear-cut profile quickly, some faint inflection in his voice warning her not to pursue the subject, yet she found she couldn't leave it alone. 'I wondered,' she said.

For one heart-stopping moment Jason turned his head and looked at her, a quick blaze behind his eyes visible even through the darkness. 'Wondered, but not worried,' he taunted. 'I thought you might be waiting that evening to congratulate me.'

'But I'd gone . . .'

'Yes, Amanda, you'd gone.'

And devil take you, his tone seemed to say, telling her all she needed to know. He was not a man to be ignored, to be rejected without explanation. By doing so she had committed an unforgivable crime. He might demand—and receive, his pound of flesh, but afterwards would come her own inexorable rejection. His eyes told her clearly, he might have spoken the message aloud! Suddenly miserable, Amanda huddled back in her soft leather seat, feeling near to tears.

At Newton Hall Richard and Eva waited. 'Why, Jason,' Eva exclaimed, as she caught sight of Amanda, 'you've worked a miracle!' Her eyes lit up with excited animation.

110

She obviously didn't notice the paleness of Amanda's face.

The corners of Jason's mouth quirked as he replied. 'It only needed a little gentle persuasion, or perhaps when I asked she was too polite to refuse.'

Eva fussed as if Amanda was two years old. 'It's the first step that counts. She'll be all right now.'

'You have my word for it.' Smoothly enigmatical, Jason removed Amanda's wrap and passed it to Eva. 'For my trouble she had promised me the first dance.'

His ill-humour apparently forgotten, he whirled her away, or perhaps it was still there in the faint pressure of his hands. Amanda resisted their insistence fretfully. 'You don't have to talk as if I wasn't around—and I don't remember promising you anything.'

'Not in so many words, but you did allow that you owed me something.'

She winced. He twisted words and people with a devious cunning. Small wonder he was reputed to be clever! 'I don't follow,' she protested breathlessly.

He murmured easily, 'I'll give you time, Amanda. Myself, I'm always in too much of a hurry.' His tingling grip tightened with disturbing intimacy, and she gasped as she thought she understood. There had been another occasion when he had used almost those exact words.

'Please,' she choked, pulling away from him, refusing to let herself even think about it. 'I'm hungry, could we try and find some supper?'

Amanda moved prettily. With her head back, her dark hair and blue eyes shining, she was eye-catching in a subtle, tantalizing way. She had a fragile beauty, an untouched air about her combined with an unconsciously sensuous movement of body which drew many masculine eyes. If she wasn't aware of it, Jason Meade was. For a while after supper he left her alone, observing her social success from a distance before taking her home.

Richard and Eva had left early, but insisted that Amanda stayed on. 'Jason will look after you,' Richard said.

An hour later Jason dropped her off at Combe Farm,

depositing her neatly on the doorstep. 'You didn't find that such an ordeal,' he suggested.

'I enjoyed myself,' she admitted reluctantly, 'very much. Thank you—er—Jason, for bringing me home.'

'Thank you, Amanda,' he said softly, and departed.

Just like that! Amanda, having let herself in, stood for a long moment with her back against the door, a cool shudder running down her spine. He really was the most unpredictable man!

## CHAPTER SEVEN

A finer spell of weather tempted Amanda to explore. This, and an unusual restlessness which had been with her since she had gone to the dance with Jason Meade. He hadn't been near her since, and that was almost a week ago, but when she mentioned this to Eva, Eva merely said that he was a busy man and would no doubt be giving them a ring before long. Amanda hadn't noticed the quick glance which had accompanied these apparently indifferent words.

She put on a jacket over her jeans and went down to the river. Previously, because of Jason, she had only dared peep at it from over the rough stone boundary wall, but now that the need for secrecy in that direction could be dispensed with, she walked boldly across the uneven ground towards it.

Away from the house all was quiet. There was no sound to be heard but a raven's croak and the river. She could hear the sound of running water long before she topped the rise and scrambled down through the dark ranks of conifers which clothed its banks. The setting was decorative, the river running down a narrow gorge but sweeping in wide curves, the water swirling into deep pools from rocky shallows. Amanda could see at once it would be an asset to any hotel, especially a sporting one. Long stretches of gravel edged the river, and here and there flat slabs of rock would provide a seat from where an angler's wife might watch her husband's performance. Shelter, too, would be provided from the variety of trees. Well hidden from the road, it afforded complete privacy. It was tailor-made for the job!

Amanda sat for a while on one of the flat rocks herself, contemplating the water. It ran dark, as though the recent snow and rain had brought flood water from other parts of the moor. Richard said flood water came down in torrents during a rainy spell. Some of the pools looked dangerously deep, deep enough to swim in, in summer. For many hotel guests this stretch of river would provide a great attraction, and she wondered why Jason hadn't already purchased it, regardless of price.

The day, though fine, didn't pretend to be anything else but late autumn. It was too cold to sit pondering. Amanda scrambled to her feet, walking quickly, trying to warm up. She had sat too long. She followed the rough track as it wound through the valley, liking the remoteness, the feeling of solitude. Above her the sky suggested rain, but she took no notice until huge drops began to fall, pattering noisily on to the tinder-dry leaves around her feet, warning her that she could get wet if she didn't soon find shelter. Knowing she must be near Jason's hotel, Amanda ran on. In her pocket she had a few coppers, enough to purchase some coffee, to provide her with an excuse to wait until the downpour was over.

To her relief she had only a few hundred yards to go. Rounding a corner, she came upon it, a huge castle-like building standing in tree-lined grounds. The size and graceful proportions of it caused her to stop for a moment and gasp. Trust Jason Meade to have only that which was pleasing to the eye! The trees looked exotic, as if some of them had been transplanted from foreign lands, the lawns, even at this time of the year, a beautiful emerald green. And, at the end of the pink-gravelled drive, stood a galaxy of smart cars in a variety of sizes. A place which undoubtedly spelt luxury in large capital letters. Not a place for a girl in a pair of tattered jeans and an even shabbier jacket. Smiling half ruefully to herself, Amanda ran lightly up the wide front steps into the foyer. Were all Jason's hotels, she wondered, like this one?

She ordered coffee and sat down in the well upholstered lounge, disregarding the slightly supercilious stare of the man who served her. She sympathised with his feelings, she did look a bit disreputable, but she hadn't expected to come so far. The weather had been wholly responsible, and she could do nothing about that. Lazily she relaxed, sipping her coffee, staring fitfully out at the rain which had developed into a steady stream, looking as if it was in for the day.

Then a voice hailed her as she gazed through the window. Surprised, she glanced around. It was one of the young men whom she had danced with at Newton Hall. She couldn't even remember his name, but he had a better memory.

'Miss Trent—Amanda!' he exclaimed. 'I was just going to give you a ring. Since the dance I've been away. I've only just returned.'

'You're . . . ?'

'Jeff Ronson,' he supplied, laughing as she hesitated. 'Can I join you for coffee?' Taking her assent for granted he rang the bell and sat down. 'I live not far from here,' he explained, 'but got caught in the rain. I detest getting wet.'

'So do I,' Amanda smiled—and he smiled back. At least, she thought wryly, they had something in common.

Jeff was pleasant. He was undemanding and easy to talk to and in his company Amanda relaxed. There was none of the tension she felt with Jason. Jeff was a light-hearted boy, not much older than herself, and very like some of the boys she had met in America. There was nothing complicated here, unless he was to take her too seriously, and she must ensure he did not. He had a nice face and good manners and asked her a few questions, but mostly chatted about himself.

She was laughing with him, at a joke he'd told well, when Jason walked in. He came with another man, his manager by the look of him. A porter hovered behind. Jason was stylishly dressed in a high-necked black sweater and a matching black leather jacket. His clothes were perfectly cut and he was impeccably groomed. He looked virile and handsome and drew many women's eyes. He saw Amanda and stopped, walking straight towards her.

'Good morning, Amanda,' he said, his eyes flicking her companion. 'To what do we owe the honour of your visit?'

Amanda flushed, hating her inability to match his coolness, and Jason's mood was cool—she sensed it. Nor did he approve of Jeff, she felt this too, but thought it none of his business. So she murmured a polite good morning, and nothing more.

He appeared to know the young man by her side, and his next words confirmed it. 'Haven't you anything better to do with your time, Jeff?' he asked. 'I saw your father yesterday. He seems far from well.'

It was Jeff's turn to flush, but sullenly. 'I'm only having a quick coffee with Amanda, Mr Meade. I do happen to be about my father's business.'

'Then you'd be wise to continue, I think,' Jason retorted crisply. 'I'll see to it that Amanda has everything she needs.'

To Amanda's astonishment Jeff rose, staring at her rather sheepishly. She couldn't understand his attitude—unless, of course, he worked for Jason. He said, 'I'd better run along, Amanda, but don't forget, you did promise to have dinner with me one evening. I'll give you a ring.'

Eyes wide, Amanda watched him go. What right did Jason have to interfere? She tried to whip up some indignation at his effrontery in daring to accost her like this, to say nothing of the way in which he'd practically ordered Jeff from the hotel! Words, however, died in her throat. She found herself unable to utter them. She had longed to see Jason and now he was here. She couldn't bear to send him away, just like that.

Scowling, he looked after Jeff's retreating figure, then he turned to his manager and introduced him briefly.

The man bowed deferentially, but there was a gleam of curiosity in his eyes as he looked at Amanda. Jason said curtly, 'You can send some fresh coffee. I'll see you later.'

Nervously Amanda blinked as he settled himself down beside her. Now that the others had gone she wasn't at all sure she wanted to be alone with him. Jeff had been a welcome change, so cheerful with his inconsequential chatter, and although she couldn't remember agreeing to have dinner with him, it might be good fun to do so. It might take her mind off other things she didn't want to think about.

Jason pulled a chair nearer to her own, pouring the fresh coffee when it arrived, but remaining silent until she turned her head to look at him. 'Ah, that's better,' he smiled, as their eyes met.

Quickly Amanda glanced away again. When Jason smiled like that he was hard to resist, although at times she suspected it was a calculated art, and had nothing to do with his real feelings. He loosened the belt of his jacket, undoing the top buttons. The clothes he wore suited him. There was a distinction about him which made her instantly aware of her own casual dress. Did any man really appreciate a girl in trousers? She became acutely conscious of her unruly appearance; her hair straggling damply around her face; her skin devoid of make-up, apart from a smear of lipstick which the rain had probably washed from her lips. Tentatively she ran the tip of her tongue over them in a rather futile attempt to find out.

'Amanda!' The firm note in his voice brought her attention back sharply. 'You might stop day-dreaming and tell me how you come to be here. I'm assuming you didn't arrive with Jeff Ronson, if he was sharing your coffee?'

Amanda winced, trying hard to retain a studied indifference. Her chin lifted as she glanced at him distantly. 'That surely isn't any of your business, Jason. Nor was it, I think, your prerogative to send Jeff away like a criminal!'

'Must we discuss Jeff Ronson? On closer acquaintance, my dear, he doesn't improve. You'd only be disappointed.'

'Well—he's a man, is he not?' She hadn't meant to put it like that.

'If that's all you want . . .'

She flushed. 'That wasn't quite what I intended. You confuse me! I don't mean that way.'

He laughed, his eyes derisive on her hot face. 'I think you do need a man, Amanda, but all in good time. And not one like Jeff. I'm sure fate will be kinder.'

'You seem to know him well!' Her voice rang with light sarcasm. It was futile to persist, but why should Jason have it all his own way? She wasn't a member of his staff, to be ordered at will, to be told what she could or could not do!

Jason's dark brows drew together and he ran an impatient hand around the back of his neck. 'His father is an old friend, afflicted with bad health. Young Jeff doesn't pull his weight. His father runs a good business, and he's supposed to help more than he does.'

'I see——' Amanda said, but didn't. What Jason told her might be true, but it still seemed no reason why Jeff should obey him immediately. But she wasn't all that interested in Jeff. It was this man sitting so near her who seemed able to set her pulses racing, to cause her heart to start beating in the most unpredictable manner.

Jason leaned forward. 'And if it's an evening out you fancy, how about having dinner with me? I'll take you to Torquay. I have another hotel down there which I'd like to show you. You can be ready about six.'

'Thank you, but no,' Amanda gasped, wholly defensive, not stopping to think. 'You don't have to take me anywhere.'

'If it's necessary then I must,' he replied, his green eyes meeting hers enigmatically. 'If I didn't do things in the proper manner, later on you might feel cheated. A girl like you, Amanda, tempts a man to use every short cut he knows.'

'I don't need to be reminded!' she gasped at his effrontery.

'You shouldn't have to be reminded of anything,' he agreed coolly. 'You should remember enough to think it wiser to do as I ask without a lot of wearisome argument. You'll be ready tomorrow at six, which should give you time to cancel any arrangements you might already have made.'

With a further denial on the tip of her tongue she hesitated. His eyes were hard, he was making it quite clear that he didn't intend to waive his hold over her. Why he should continue to bother with her at all she couldn't think. She had imagined that after the ball at Newton Hall his interest would die. He was older than she was and much more

118

sophisticated. Beside him she felt naïve, unable to understand the attraction between them, or how to cope with it.
Perhaps like Veronica, he was using her as a means of ac-
cess to the river, yet her mind shied away from such a suggestion, reluctant to believe it. At least she knew enough to
keep her head, and if he was determined to entertain her,
she could take whatever he offered with a clear conscience,
without feeling in any way compelled to give him anything
in return.

So she checked herself and, after a long moment, said
primly, 'You haven't given me much time, but I'll do my
best.'

'I hope so, Amanda,' he said dryly, apparently taking her
acquiescence for granted.

'Whatever do you mean?'

He looked pointedly at her tight shirt. 'You don't try to
enhance yourself. If you've nothing better to wear than the
dress you wore at Newton, then you'd better go out and get
yourself something.'

Scarlet, she flushed. 'You really have a nerve,' she flashed
tautly. 'I'll wear what I like!'

'Then I had better like it too,' he rejoined, with the uttermost coolness, 'or I won't answer for the consequences.'

She raised her brows. 'Indeed?'

'Indeed,' he snapped, leaving her in no doubt as to who
was the master. 'Wear that old white chiffon and I'll rip it
off in two minutes—maybe less if you try me too far. And
I'm quite capable of it, you know.'

Understandably Amanda never properly remembered her
journey from the hotel back to Combe Farm. Jason sent her
home in style, refusing to let her walk. After his last out-
rageous remark about her dress, she had jumped up and
left him, almost bumping into his manager as she had
turned to go. While the man had whispered to Jason that an
urgent call awaited him in the office, she had made her escape, only to find herself followed by one of the porters,
complete with instructions from Mr Meade to drive her
home. Unable to find a suitable excuse, especially in the face

of the driving rain, she could do nothing else but accept.

Still seething with rage, in spite of a peculiar excitement, she was determined to ignore what Jason said. It had been unpardonable of him to make such an attack on her person. He had no right—or rights; she was not sure which. She probably meant both. Muddled thoughts hurtling through her brain, she ran upstairs, surprised, minutes later, to find herself rummaging despairingly through her wardrobe, considering the row of drab-looking dresses hanging there. She possessed nothing, she was sure, that Jason would approve of.

Minutes later, Eva found her. 'Are you looking for anything special, darling?' she asked.

Amanda let her frown stay where it was. 'I'm going out for dinner,' she confessed without meaning to, 'and my escort has requested I wear something decent!' Which wasn't quite how Jason had put it, but just about summed it up.

'Oh, dear . . .' Eva blinked, mildly startled. 'Well, that's certainly an original approach. I must admit, myself, I didn't think much of that rather jaded white chiffon. But who is the man, darling? I would like to know.'

Abruptly Amanda told her, not caring for the amused curiosity in Eva's voice. 'And I've a good mind to wear my white chiffon again,' she added sulkily. 'Veronica gave it to me when I left school. I haven't worn it more than twice.'

'Once too often, then,' Eva said tartly. 'I certainly wouldn't advise you to wear it again. Not for Jason. It wouldn't do. Where have you seen him, by the way?' she queried in a rush.

Amanda sighed, patiently. She had expected Eva to ask. 'It rained while I was out this morning, and I took shelter in the hotel. He came in.'

'Just like that?' Eva peered over Amanda's shoulder, visibly impressed. 'And you looking a perfect little tramp, darling,' she laughed. 'We must convince him you can do better.' She pointed to the nylon jersey. 'Jason might like that.'

The suppressed eagerness in Eva's voice caused Amanda

to glance at her suspiciously. Surely they weren't hoping she would carry on where Veronica had left off? Unless Jason mentioned it himself, she had no intention of discussing the river. Richard must do his own negotiating in that direction.

Quickly—too quickly, she said, 'What Jason thinks is not important, but I might run into town this afternoon and buy some shoes, if I could borrow the car? The shops were just closing when I brought this dress. I didn't have time to get any new ones.'

She could borrow the car any time, Eva assured her, and of course, Amanda had to ask if she would like to come with her.

'Oh, that would be lovely!' Eva was delighted. 'I do need a few things myself. We can shop together.'

In Newton Abbot Amanda had her hair done. It was Eva's idea, but Amanda knew her hair needed cutting and shaping. Though it was growing nicely longer, there was bound to be a lot of split ends. Besides, it was nice to sit beneath the drier and dream, cocooned in a soft, warm world where no one could reach her.

Later Eva insisted firmly that Amanda must have a new wrap. 'The one you have belonged to Veronica,' she said keenly. 'I recognised it. Don't you have anything of your own?'

'Of course,' Amanda smiled lightly. 'But Veronica leads a very social life. Lots of her things are not even shabby when she throws them out.'

'Your sister,' retorted Eva, 'can discard as she pleases, but you aren't obliged to accept everything she offers. You aren't the same size. You'd have to cut most of her things down.'

'A little . . .' Amanda admitted.

'A lot!' Eva sniffed.

Finally Amanda went home with a lovely jacket in imitation mink, a present from Eva, along with a pair of silvery evening slippers and a new bag. She ought, she thought wryly, to look extremely smart. Smart enough to satisfy

Jason, maybe? She pretended to be delighted, to please Eva, but her heart in no way reflected the sparkle in her eyes.

Jason arrived early the following evening. He had contacted her that morning by telephone and asked if she would accompany him after dinner to the house of a friend. There was some business which was suddenly important. Amanda had agreed, feeling she had little other option, but not at all sure she really wanted to go. For this one evening she hadn't wanted to share Jason with anyone, but then he was not to know.

There was a moon that evening, sailing high in the heavens—not a very full one, but enough to cast a romantic glow. Amanda saw it as she went to the door in answer to Jason's ring. Richard insisted she asked him in for a drink before they set off, and reluctantly she had agreed.

This evening Amanda wore her bluey-green dress which suited her graceful figure, and reflected the blue of her eyes. The radiant image which her mirror reflected satisfied her that for this one night at least Jason should have no complaint. The colours enhanced the faint tan which she still had from her trip abroad, giving a fine glow to her skin which she hadn't previously noticed. Her hair looked wonderful. Eva's hairdresser was certainly expert! It was straight and heavy, long enough to coil into a knot at the nape of her neck, a simplicity of style which suited her regular features and showed the perfect shape of her head. As on that other evening when she had gone to Newton Hall, she applied a trace of eye-shadow, a hint of colour to her lips. A slight shiver ran through her as she had realised how much she was looking forward to dining alone with Jason. Not even the prospect of having to share him afterwards could dim a glowing anticipation.

Jason, in a dinner jacket, was impressive, and when she opened the door and he saw her standing there, her dress gleaming against the shadows behind her, he stood quite still for a moment staring, while a slow fire kindled in his eyes.

Amanda evaded that brilliant glance as best she could, not

ready yet to give way to a quiver of primitive awareness. With a trace of breathlessness she dropped him a defiant curtsey, her lashes flickering on to lightly powdered cheeks. 'Will I do?'

He came forward and took her arm. 'Quite an improvement,' he teased, 'although you never were an ugly duckling.'

'Nor am I yet a swan, I suppose,' she answered sharply, freeing herself from his hold before his grip could tighten. The mocking note in his voice hurt, as did his soft arrogance. 'Richard would like you to have a drink before we go,' she added hastily.

Richard looked tired and confessed that he felt a little weary. 'I'm getting on, I'm afraid,' he grinned ruefully. 'I'm finding travelling more of a strain than I used to. One of these trips will have to be my last.'

'That will be the day!' Eva laughed, but Amanda thought Eva might, underneath her lightheartedness, be rather worried. Richard was quiet, preoccupied, inclined to be forgetful. Nothing new in this, Amanda supposed, but one couldn't discount a subtle change in him.

She said as much to Jason as they left. Between them there existed some pretence of friendship, enough for her to mention Richard to him casually.

Jason replied briefly, but with some authority. 'Your father has always lived in a world of his own, and as he gets older he'll retreat further. Like many dedicated men he's totally absorbed in his work. You might be thankful for Eva. She bridges the gap between his world and ours. Otherwise he might lose touch altogether.'

'I'm glad he's got Eva,' Amanda said simply, but with absolute sincerity.

Momentarily he turned his head sideways, his vivid glance sliding over her. 'You're full of concern, yet you never choose to come down here yourself. Your sister came, but you stayed in London. Once I remember wondering why?'

'I happened to be in America!' Stung, she retorted

123

sharply. Suddenly she realised he had mentioned Veronica. Here was the opportunity she had waited for. It should be easy, now, to ask how well he had known Veronica, yet she found herself unable to do so. Perhaps she didn't want to know the answer which must surely fall from his lips. In order to cover a slight hesitation, she felt forced to explain further. 'I was in Florida over two years. Previous to that I was at school and stayed with Veronica during school holidays, and after I left.'

'Two years was a long time.'

Lulled by the light neutrality in his voice, Amanda went on, innocently satisfying his curiosity, 'It didn't seem a long time. There was so much to do, and everything was different. I only intended staying for a short while to begin with, but the people I went with had twin boys, and I grew attached to them. Actually we had great fun. Their parents, like my father, were too busy to bother much, and the twins were used to me. I could never bring myself to leave them.'

'But you did in the end.'

'Yes, it was a sudden decision . . .'

'There is usually a reason?'

She retorted stubbornly, 'There doesn't always have to be.' He would only laugh if she confessed to feeling that life was passing her by. She hoped her negative reply had dampened his interest.

But he persisted, if idly, 'I believe you were returning to America with your sister. What was the attraction?'

In the darkness Amanda squirmed uncomfortably, though why she was not sure. It could have, she realised, something to do with Herman. She was well aware that in her own mind she had allowed the incident with Herman to assume unreasonable proportions. He hadn't touched her, even if that had been his intention, but now even to think of him made her feel besmirched in some way. 'There was no attraction,' she said carefully. 'You see, I'd lived with Veronica since Daddy married again—we thought it best, at the time. But Veronica sold the flat after Herman finished his tour of duty. I had nowhere to go.'

'Didn't you feel a bit de trop? After all, they'd only been married three months. Couldn't you have managed on your own?'

His voice had hardened again. Quite clearly he considered girls who couldn't fend for themselves spineless. Well, she didn't want his sympathy, but nor would she accept his contempt. She couldn't tell him the whole story, and, momentarily, she was glad, when he was being so disagreeable about the innocent little bit he knew. 'Veronica begged me to go with her,' she replied stiffly. 'I found it impossible to refuse. Besides,' she added tonelessly, 'I hadn't enough money to find a flat of my own, and I had no job to help me get one.'

'Veronica had money of her own,' he said disagreeably.

'Yes, I know. But she had a good job, and money which our mother left her.'

'Your mother?'

'Yes ... You see, she died, as you probably know, when I was born, and a few years previously she'd left everything she had to Veronica. I was a sort of surprise packet, you see, not expected. Daddy said afterwards she probably intended to change her will later, but she didn't have time.'

'And Veronica never offered you a share?'

'Not money-wise—but she did give me a home when I needed one, and was always good to me.'

'And what made you change your mind about going to America again?' His voice slowed to a drawl, as if he sifted and assessed what she told him in his mind like a mathematical problem, sure of his ability to arrive at the correct answer.

Amanda clutched nervously at the edge of her seat, reminding herself to be careful. How easy it was, when travelling like this at night, to let one's tongue betray too many secrets! The road slid swiftly and smoothly by, the effect hypnotic. Jason was controlling her thoughts, his voice playing on her senses in a calculating, attractive fashion, and puppet-like she was responding. This was the hold he had over her, and she would do well to be aware of it. He wanted to know why she hadn't gone to America. It might be wise to satisfy his curiosity, but she hated him for probing. 'I guess Veronica and I fell out,' she sighed. 'Nothing unusual in that—for sisters.'

'But you'd already planned to go? You must have had one whale of a quarrel. What about?'

'I suddenly decided not to. Can't we leave it at that?' Her voice rose, slightly hysterical as the whole disturbing incident returned to haunt her. She could never tell Jason the truth, nor was it necessary. Surely he must realise she didn't want to talk about it? It wasn't as if it was interesting. She couldn't think why he bothered. Yet a few seconds later she thought she knew why.

'Do you think Veronica is happy?' he queried, ignoring her plea indifferently. 'Herman appears a nice enough chap, but, I imagine, easily led astray.'

Hot and cold Amanda went by turns. His sympathy was obviously with Veronica, and his summing up of Herman accurate to a degree. So accurate, in fact, that should Veronica ever relate the story of Amanda's fall from grace, Jason would have no difficulty at all in believing! He was worrying about Veronica's marriage. Why else would he inquire after her happiness? Amanda's lower lip trembled slightly and she bit on it. 'I expect she's happy,' she murmured, not very truthfully. 'She certainly seems to be.'

She fell silent after that and Jason too became preoccupied, the set of his mouth a little grim, he did not speak again until they ran into Torquay. Jason parked the car in front of the hotel where they were to dine, but before they went in he walked with her a little way until they could see the sea. Even in the moonlight the setting was panoramic. From where they stood amongst the high wooded hills overlooking Tor Bay, the lights of the town twinkled gaily. And below them anchored boats could plainly be seen bobbing gently up and down on the water. Amanda, who had never been here before, felt impressed. The sub-tropical trees and flowers in the garden beside them could almost make her imagine she was back in Florida, and she could smell the sea in the pine-scented air about them.

Jason, by her side with a protective hand beneath her elbow, added to the magic of the still, dark night, but confused her mind effectively. All she could think of to say was, 'In summer this must all be very attractive, almost Continental.'

Jason laughed. 'Torquay's popularity as a holiday resort dates from the nineteenth century, when the Napoleonic wars prevented many well-off people from taking a holiday on the Continent. Times have changed slightly since then, mostly, I imagine, because of our inclement weather, but during a hot summer such as we've just had, I think we might have been almost as busy as the South of France.'

'I must come and see for myself,' she said.

He shrugged. 'I think you would like it. It has everything to offer.'

'Yet you go abroad,' she glanced at him quickly.

'I do,' he replied, his eyebrow quirking. 'I suspect you've been gossiping with Mrs Drew?' He smiled again as he felt a small tremor shoot through her, confirming his suspicions. 'I go to France and Spain chiefly because I have property development out there. But I do have one or two special spots, Amanda, which I might show you one day.'

As usual he was teasing. 'I'd better see something of Devon first,' she retorted, to hide the faster beating of her heart as he took her back to the hotel.

'Not many ever explore the county in which they live,' he rejoined mildly, yet slanting her a wicked look as though he knew exactly how she was feeling.

If the appearance of the foyer was anything to go by, this hotel was just as luxurious as his other one on Dartmoor. Pretending great interest, she stared around, in order to hide her flushed cheeks, but his keen eyes noted her heightened colour. 'Am I rushing you, Amanda?' he queried softly. 'Because I mean to—so you'd better be warned.'

She tossed her head like an obstinate child, refusing to understand, pretending not to hear the veiled threat in his voice as he spoke, but finding it impossible to evade his gaze for long. Green eyes, faintly cynical, looked down, pinning her own with deliberate concentration. With a desperate effort she pulled herself together. 'At times I find it difficult to understand you,' she said frostily, and with as much dignity as she could muster.

For a moment his eyes darkened. It seemed he was about to add something more, then suddenly decided to let it go. It was time to eat, and there would be time—plenty of time, later. Some sensitive part of Amanda knew this and reacted strangely, not surprised when he muttered softly that a hotel foyer was scarcely the place to pursue such matters. Their dinner was waiting.

As on Dartmoor, the manager hovered in the background, along with a retinue of staff, all very unobtrusive, but there, none the less. Wistfully Amanda wished they could have gone somewhere quieter, where perhaps Jason wasn't so well known. The curious if discreet glances cast in her direction didn't appear to worry him, but she hated to feel herself the centre of such interest, and felt resentful that he had subjected her to it.

Once they were seated, however, she forgot about the others and continued to look around her. After all, this was Jason's hotel, why should he go to the additional expense of taking her elsewhere? The place was busy, and when she expressed astonishment he assured her that if it wasn't busy, even at this time of the year, he would want to know the reason why.

'I thought you didn't work during the winter,' she said.

'I don't,' he agreed, 'but I get around. Occasionally a crisis blows up.'

'Such as yesterday morning?' she asked.

'Something like that,' he nodded. 'I might be at Merington, but I'm always available.'

The meal Jason chose was delicious, but Amanda could never afterwards remember exactly what she ate. She was too conscious of Jason sitting opposite her, and could not but be aware that he gave her his whole attention, rarely taking his eyes from her face. He even went so far as to

128

cover her hand with his while they waited between courses.

As if he was perfectly aware of the effect he was having, his fingers tightened over her quivering ones as, startled, she tried to draw them away. Quickly, still holding her, he turned her hand over in his. 'You have beautiful hands, Amanda,' he said lazily, his eyes examining her smooth, delicate fingers. 'With hands like these you ought to sit on a cushion and sew a fine seam, all day.'

'Hardly practical for a modern miss,' she said in a soft, shaky voice. His hand was warm and hard and excitement thrummed along her veins.

'But you're not duty bound to be a modern miss, are you, Amanda? Although you certainly look one in that dress.' His eyes slid over her, teasing yet intent on her slender figure, her silky skin. 'You look quite beautiful this evening, Amanda,' he said.

Despite the warmth of the room, for no definable reason that she could think of Amanda shivered, her heavy lashes falling even while she suddenly longed for the sophistication to hold his insistent glance. Her dress was a success, she was aware of it. It left her arms and shoulders bare and showed the alluring curve of her breast, the slender span of her waist. In it she felt she was someone quite different from her usual self. A faint sense of strain took possession of her. Perhaps she had had too much wine? She wasn't used to drinking a lot of wine, just a little of this or that occasionally. It had to be the wine, this floating, out of this world sensation which seemed to scatter the few remaining inhibitions she had left. In some ridiculous fashion she was even beginning to like the way he continued to hold her hand lightly, and allowed her own fingers to curl experimentally around his, not willing that this incredible magic should desert her, floating luminously on the tantalizing wave of her drifting emotions.

It was only as the waiter approached their table with the sweet that Jason spoke again in a gentle, tolerant voice, and she aroused herself, her wide blue eyes startled. Quickly breathless, she straightened, returning his smile, faintly apologetic, yet managing to retain an admirable cool in spite of the colour that crept under her smooth skin. 'I think I was almost asleep,' she said lightly.

A glitter of something she could not put a name to crossed his dark watching face. 'Well, at least your dreams appeared to be pleasant,' he drawled, the quirk at the corner of his well-shaped mouth proclaiming him not the smallest bit impressed by her untruthfulness.

# CHAPTER EIGHT

It was very pleasant in the hotel, the food, service and decor all being first class, but they did not linger long after they had finished eating. They didn't in fact stay for coffee. Jason told her that his friend's house was some half-hour's drive away, and somehow Amanda sensed he was keen to be off. He wasn't a man to give much away, but this evening she was aware, or thought she was, of an underlying eagerness, slightly perplexing in a man who usually controlled his emotions to a fine degree.

Nor was she proved wrong. 'David Hartley has a young mare,' he explained, as they drove out of Torquay. 'She's only four years old and I've had my eye on her for some time, but he's always refused to sell. Now it seems that circumstances have forced him to change his mind. This is why he rang me this morning.'

'Wouldn't he be better to sell at auction?' Amanda asked, glancing at Jason quickly but feeling a renewed stirring of interest. She had liked his horses, the atmosphere of his stables, and had found herself wishing more than once since she had left Merington that it might have been possible to have a horse of her own at Combe Farm. But of course the land there was all rented out, and besides, she could scarcely afford one. Jason had quite a number of horses and she wondered suddenly why he should want more. And why the subdued excitement about one particular mare? Something, a small flicker of she knew not what, went through her—an uneasy moment which she cast hastily aside. It wasn't possible to be jealous of a horse! She might have asked him to teach her to ride, but this she realized would be far from practical. Jason Meade was a busy man. If she had doubted it before, she had learnt enough during the past few days to convince her otherwise. He could not possibly have time to spare for such idle pursuits as she had in mind.

Through the tangle of her wistful thoughts she heard him answering her question. 'He might get a better price on the open market, but then again he might not. He couldn't actually hope to better what I'm offering for the horse, and I believe he wants to sell privately. There is, however, another man who is interested. This is why I should like to complete the deal this evening.'

Amanda asked, greatly daring, 'Why should you want another horse? You can't surely ride them all.'

'Do I detect a note of censure?' he laughed, but gently, turning his head to glance at her averted profile.

'Perhaps it's envy . . .' She laughed lightly with him. She didn't pretend to know anything about horses, but she did know that when Jason talked about them he seemed much more relaxed.

Steadily the car wound its way through the dark Devonshire lanes which stretched tunnel-like before them, between high hedges. The headlights flung strange, leaping shadows across the road, reminding Amanda once again of the pagan tales of Dartmoor. An owl flew alongside the car, then swooped away again silently. From a nearby field came a fox, its long, bushy tail trailing behind it and with what looked suspiciously like a pheasant or a chicken in its mouth. Apparently not at all alarmed by the beam of car lights, it turned to trot up the side of the road, waiting it seemed for them to pass before continuing on its journey.

Jason said dryly, as if perfectly aware of her doubts, 'I don't just ride horses, Amanda, I breed and sell them. Horses were my first line of business—they might even be my last. At least they have never let me down.'

There was some intangible quality in his voice not easily assimilated. A small frown passed quickly over Amanda's smooth forehead. If he had been anyone else but Jason Meade she might have concluded that some woman had been unfaithful. More likely, she thought cynically, it would be the other way around. Veronica, of course, according to Eva, had loved him and left him—high and dry! Yet somehow Amanda doubted this very much. When it

132

came to loving and leaving it would be Jason who called the tune.

The thought filled her with a strange resentment, an unrealistic indignation that this should be so, and she felt oddly relieved when they turned in between high, pillared gates, arriving swiftly before the huge front door of a large, ivy-clad house. If Jason had expected some comment on his last remark he would have to be disappointed.

The house was far from the quiet country establishment she had been anticipating. Lights poured from every window along with the sound of gay music. 'It looks as if they're having a party,' Jason muttered. 'Janetta, David's wife, is fond of them. Too fond,' he added sourly, but again enigmatically, without explanation.

Leaving the car, Amanda followed him rather reluctantly inside, feeling, in spite of Jason's protective presence, something of a gatecrasher. The place seemed alive with people, all apparently having a good time, and after introducing her to their hostess, a petite blonde with a lively disposition, Jason left her with a drink in her hand and did not return again for well over an hour. And when he did come back, he chose not to stay any longer. Ignoring, with easy charm, the entreaties of the glamorous Janetta, he took Amanda away, the pressure of his fingers on her arm implying that it would be useless to plead she would have liked to remain for a while. She had danced a little, and, being young, had enjoyed it. It would have been nice to dance again with Jason, but obviously he had no such inclinations.

But if her own mood was despondent because of their swift departure, his was quite the opposite. 'I've got her,' he said with a quick grin, as they drove away. 'Come over to Merington tomorrow, Amanda, and see her. David promises to deliver in the morning. You'll like her, she's superb!'

There was no mistaking the enthusiasm in Jason's voice, but if Amanda felt impressed by his successful purchase she pretended not to be so. She ignored what he said about going to Merington. 'You left me in a roomful of strangers,' she retorted coolly. 'You can't really expect congratulations!'

'Was it so unforgivable, Amanda?' He flashed her a quick look, his good mood still holding. 'I'll admit I didn't expect to be gone so long, but these things take time, and I didn't think you would miss me. Besides,' he added, with a quirk at the side of his well-cut lips, 'you did find one familiar face amongst the throng. Didn't I see Jeff Ronson making his way in your direction as I went out with David?'

'You don't know that I wanted to see him all that much,' she protested. 'I scarcely know him. But it was,' she conceded with some bitterness, 'a good job he was there.'

'Well, at least you didn't come to any harm . . .'

'I'm not sure.' Beneath his total disregard, Amanda moved fretfully, clinging stubbornly to a little feminine imperviousness. 'I think I've had too much to drink. Jeff kept bringing me something which seemed fairly harmless at the time, but now I seem to feel a bit peculiar.'

Jason laughed with seeming indifference. 'I shouldn't think it's done irreparable harm, but all the more reason to be grateful that I rescued you. If you sit back and relax I think you'll soon find yourself returning to normal. And don't forget my invitation to Merington while you're dreaming of Jeff Ronson.'

Jason could be impossible when he so chose! Yet somehow Amanda felt herself doing as she was told, although she found it impossible to relax completely. 'I must see about a job,' she was surprised to hear herself saying slowly. 'Do you still have a vacancy in one of your hotels?'

'Right at this moment, no,' he replied, after a moment's silence. 'For the time being I'd advise you to stay where you are.'

'But you offered me one, if you remember?'

'When I imagined your circumstances were entirely different.'

'But I can't stay at Combe Farm for ever, doing nothing,' she cried.

'You help Eva.' The lightness had left his voice and his

134

tone was discouraging.

She threw him a swift, frowning look through the darkness. How did he know about that, or was he only guessing? 'Eva can get plenty of help. In fact, I believe I'm doing her daily out of a job, but I have to do something to justify my keep.'

'I'm sure neither your father or Eva would begrudge you that,' he said firmly.

Something—some inflection in his voice, made Amanda see red. 'I would like to be able to contribute towards general expenses, which is not what I'm doing now. Daddy is far from being a wealthy man.' Turning in her seat, she stared at him tersely, as if trying to emphasize her point, a sick feeling welling in her throat. For no reason whatsoever she longed to get beneath the hard, protective veneer he wore so naturally. 'Not everyone,' she choked, 'is as well endowed as yourself. It must be pleasant to be rich, but it rarely seems to make a man more sensitive.'

'Amanda!' Suddenly impatient, he pressed his foot on the accelerator and the car leapt forward. Within seconds a side turning appeared and Jason pulled off the main road. There was a wide gravel verge beside a gateway and he drove on to it and stopped. There was little traffic about, none it seemed on this stretch of road, and the night was very still.

Amanda heard a faint click as he released his seat belt. It was too dark in the car to see his face, nor, for a moment, did she try. Blindly she stared in front of her, her eyes fixed on the distant hills whose shadowy silhouettes she could see through the wide wooden bars of the gate. Helplessly she concentrated on the blurred outlines, praying fervently that he couldn't hear the hard frantic beating of her heart. When a man stopped like this at this time of night it usually meant one thing. Not that Jason always followed the conventional pattern, but if he had wanted only to talk, he could quite easily have done so while he was driving. Perhaps it had been because he had been driving that she had dared to taunt him. Now regrets tore at her, but there seemed nothing she could say to put things right.

But when Jason spoke his voice was curiously even, and he made no attempt to touch her. 'Amanda,' he repeated dryly, his eyes penetrating the gloom, 'we seem to be at cross purposes. I merely assumed your father to be well off, that's all. A fairly innocent mistake, I can assure you.'

'You assumed!' Distraught, Amanda raged bitterly, engaging any emotion which might hide the chaos within her. 'How can you speak so glibly! You must have known he was short of money when he tried to sell you the river. You can't plead ignorance about that!'

For a moment he seemed struck into silence, and when he spoke again his voice had an increasing dryness. 'I know he wanted to sell the river, my dear, but I was under no obligation to buy it.'

'But you wanted it . . . ? You even discussed it.'

'Naturally.' He turned in his seat, easing his weight around, so that he was able more clearly to see her dim profile. 'That particular stretch of water would do the hotel no harm, but first and foremost I'm a business man, Amanda. I have a fair idea what the fishing there is worth, and I'm not prepared to give more.'

'But you might have done if . . .' Nervously Amanda's voice trailed away. She had not intended to so much as mention the river, yet here she was going even further than that! Through the utter confusion which smote her she heard him prompting silkily, 'If what, Amanda?'

'If—if you'd wanted it badly enough,' she managed, grateful that her wits hadn't deserted her completely.

From the derisive twist of his lips, there seemed little doubt he could see through her prevarication, but it became apparent that he wasn't going to challenge her immediately. He said softly, 'There happen to be several reasons why I've done nothing yet about the river, but none of them, my dear, need concern you. And if your father can't afford to keep you, Amanda, then I can.'

Surprise closed her throat, stopping all speech as she gazed back at him in helpless consternation. He was teasing her, she knew that, yet there was a look on his lean, dark face she couldn't define. Unless, of course, he was offering her a job after all—a salary? But before she could find the suitable words to ask, his hand went out to touch the fur of her jacket. 'You wouldn't have to wear imitation mink, I would buy you the real thing. Doesn't that tempt you?' he said.

'The real thing . . . ?' Fright for a moment ran through her. If she hadn't taken him seriously before, something in his eyes contradicted this former impression. He didn't move, but she felt the change in him, a sort of complex tension. She heard what he was saying but wasn't at all sure what he was on about. It must be a job—surely he wasn't asking her to live with him! Her eyes, brilliant with shock, clung to his, trying to read an expression which should have warned her. There was a confident expectancy about his waiting stillness. She felt it, even if she could not clearly discern what lay behind it. If only her heart would stop thudding so desperately, her pulse refrain from breaking all records! She drew back from him a little, the silken mesh of her hair caught in the moonlight. Her voice, when it came, was weak. 'Perhaps you could explain,' she whispered.

He gave her an odd sort of smile, only half mocking, and moved one hand to her shoulder in one of his dominating gestures. With a quick flick he pushed aside her seat belt and pulled her nerveless body into his arms, burying his face against her hair. Nothing more—but his next words deepened the shock which already held her, bringing with it total disintegration!

'I've wanted you,' he said slowly, 'ever since I carried you into Merington that night and tucked you up in bed. I've wanted you and intend to have you, even if I have to buy the damned river to get you. Surely you realized I would never let you go?'

For one startling instant all Amanda's strength seemed to leave her, although she felt herself go rigid in his arms, the coolness of his voice along with what he said taking the breath almost forcibly from her. The way in which he phrased his words alarmed her, and because she didn't reply immediately she sensed his barely suppressed impatience.

'Amanda?' he prompted tersely.

The tension mounted. 'I don't understand,' her breath came unevenly. 'You talk in riddles!'

'Riddles!' Jason echoed the word. His expression hardened. 'Trust a woman to cling to a little mystery! I'm offering you everything you could ever want and you pretend not to understand.'

'In heaven's name, then, why?' A fiery expression darkened her eyes as anger replaced the bewilderment within her. She could not analyse her feelings. He didn't speak of love, but there were so many different kinds of love; so many degrees. She remembered how after he had first discovered who she really was, he had denied having any designs on her person. Yet here he was now, almost admitting that he had had this in mind all the time. What did he expect her to do? Agree to go to Merington and live with him? Here her confused thoughts stopped. In spite of herself excitement touched her. Her own sensuous reaction to Jason Meade was not something entirely new, and her mind she found could not altogether control the instinctive impulses of her body.

The sudden silence brought a sensation of unreality as he stared at her, his dark brows drawn. She could feel his breath warm on her cheek as his head came nearer. 'Don't you know the answer, Amanda?' he asked abruptly, his hand exploring her face, tracing the line of her throat.

His mouth was but inches from her own, and to her dismay she found it impossible to turn away, not realizing until this moment how much she had longed for his kisses. Helplessly, unable to stop herself, she turned her mouth up to his and only for a second did he hesitate before pulling her closer. Then, with a smothered exclamation, he held her to him, his arms hard, his lips hurting, expertly extracting the passionate response he relentlessly sought. His touch, his kiss, his nearness seemed to spark to blazing light some dormant fire within her, and she felt her hands creep up around his neck, her body melt into his, and had no thought of denying him anything.

She scarcely felt his hands pushing her fur wrap from her shoulders, until his lips left her mouth to trail down her cheek and rest firmly on her warm, bare skin. There their increased pressure played havoc with her starved senses as deliberately it seemed he sought to punish her for some misdemeanour—she knew not what.

But when at last he moved his head she felt bereft, not able to do without the positive magic of his arms. It was like sailing amongst the stars, a mindless, crazy trip, playing with fire and not caring if she got burnt. Convulsively she moved against his shoulder, not aware of what she was saying. 'Jason,' she whispered, as his mouth came back to her face, 'please kiss me again.'

Not needing a second bidding, he moved his hand gently up to grasp a handful of her hair, not heeding her soft gasp as her head came back into his shoulder, as his lips descended unerringly again. 'Are you begging, my lovely Amanda?' he asked with gentle mockery against her softly trembling mouth.

Amanda was past words—she was all mixed up. The blood pounded through her veins and she felt suddenly full of a desperate yearning which made it impossible to fight her own turbulent desires. There seemed nothing she could do but wait until his lips crushed hers, this time not playing with half measures, but subjecting her to his hard, bruising strength, not prepared to treat her gently any more.

Tears of intensity forced their way between her tightly closed lids, finding their way to his mouth. She had known tentative, adolescent kisses. This evening, for a short while on the terrace of the house where Jason had bought his mare, she had allowed Jeff to hold her. She had even returned his kisses experimentally, mixing them up with a sort of defiant indignation that Jason should have left her for such a time. Jeff's kisses had been pleasant, oddly comforting, and she had had no objection to staying in his arms. But she had felt herself cold, too conscious of the noise about them, and it had been with a strange dissatisfaction that she had turned away. None of this touched her when Jason held her. In his arms there was all the response from her body she could ever hope for, yet irrationally this filled her with a similar dismay. Her slender fragility, her innocence made one last stand of independence. Maybe she was not ready yet for total domination, such as she would be forced to accept in Jason's arms.

She heard the deep intake of his breath as his lips left hers abruptly, as the faint saltiness of her tears penetrated and he lifted his head.

He didn't let her go. His hand came up to brush the tears from her face, to smooth the hair back from her hot cheeks as if he was perfectly aware of the emotions he aroused in her but while prepared to be gentle was not willing that she should escape. 'Marry me, Amanda,' he said softly.

Amanda's eyes flew open, staring at him through the darkness, as shock tore through her. She had never expected to hear such words pass his lips, and startled, she drew away from him, a shiver of apprehension sobering her completely. He seemed to be asking her to marry him, but he hadn't said a word about love. Yet something must have prompted his proposal. Was it the river? Did he expect that by marrying her he might get it for nothing? No—this just didn't make sense, he had enough money to buy a dozen such rivers should he so choose. But there must be something—something which might have occurred to a man of his devious nature, which she wasn't aware of herself.

Maybe, she thought rather desperately, her tears had prompted those few impulsive words, this, and an undeniable attraction which seemed to lie between them. Men had been known to marry for less. She was tempted herself. In Jason's arms she found a searing excitement and the only security she had ever known, but not yet was she experienced enough to differentiate between two such incompatible emotions, nor was she prepared to try. That she was near to loving him in a devastating and wholly unpredictable way would be no excuse for agreeing to marry a man who didn't return her feelings.

Through a daze she heard him repeating his question as she remained silent in his arms. 'Amanda,' he asked, tersely, 'didn't you hear what I was saying?'

She recoiled from the hardness of his voice, retreating into some sensitive area of her subconsciousness. He sounded as if he was arranging some business transaction! She looked up at him with a mixture of resentment. 'I couldn't marry you,' she answered, a little wildly. 'Please, Jason, take me home.'

'No!' his hands gripped her bare shoulders with unconcealed impatience, taking no notice of her pleading blue eyes. 'Surely,' he snapped harshly, 'you realize what I'm offering? What more do you want?'

'Put like that, a whole lot more!' Anger surged as her head went back defiantly. She had never thought him insensitive. Obviously the women he had dealt with until now had never evoked his more protective emotions. Neither had she, for that matter! He wanted her, but he didn't love her —so much was clear, but that he only imagined she would consider him in the terms of his wealth hurt almost beyond endurance.

'Maybe,' he taunted, his hand sliding across her silken skin, 'maybe you're not interested in marriage. Another relationship might be easily arranged, but I wouldn't want to shock your sensibilities. I've thought of you as a charming little innocent, but I have a notion I might have been mistaken.'

The silence which followed was fraught with a fine tension, the painful hurt of disillusion. Amanda felt herself go white and pulled forcibly out of his detaining arms. 'It's none of your business, Jason Meade, what sort of a girl I am! I don't owe you a thing, not even an explanation.'

'I saved your life. By every unwritten law you should belong to me—with or without a marriage ceremony,' he said coolly.

Fury smote her at that, rendering her speechless. She was well aware that for some reason he had deliberately intended to shock her. They had argued before. It was a debatable point whether he had saved her life or endangered it, but she refused to demean herself by pointing this out to him again. Her head throbbed with all the misery of shocked senses, and she sat mutely, staring at her hands.

'Amanda . . .' Suddenly, with a startling suddenness, his mood changed, and before she could stop him he pulled her back into his arms, covering her tear-damp cheeks with gentle kisses. 'Relax, girl,' he spoke softly against her lips, his hands caressing. 'Forget what we've said tonight. You're far from indifferent to me, I can sense it. I'm quite willing to wait a little longer. I'll give you all the time you could possibly want.'

Long after Jason had driven her home, Amanda tried to remember why she hadn't turned him down completely. He had been too gently persuasive, too skilled in the arts of gentle seduction, too knowledgeable as to what made a girl respond almost completely. It had been a temptation beyond her control to stay in his arms a while longer. It had only been when Jason himself had released her abruptly, as a clock in some nearby church steeple had chimed the hour of midnight, that she had realized the limits he had set, though self-imposed, were only so far controllable. But when he had dropped her on her doorstep she had still been adamant about marrying him. Never, she had told him fervently, in a hundred years. There had been little comfort to be gained from the totally sardonic smile which he had given her as he had turned away.

Next morning, not surprisingly, her head ached badly and she felt distraught. So pale was she that when she went downstairs Eva insisted she went back to bed with aspirin and a cup of hot tea. And afterwards, because she did as she was told, Amanda blamed herself for what happened.

She quite forgot that she had promised to take Richard into Exeter, and Eva didn't remind her. Eva said later she had been on her way to remind her, but Amanda had fallen asleep again and Richard, when consulted, had insisted on driving himself. After all, before Amanda had arrived he had done this all the time, and in London he had gone everywhere by car. Perhaps if there had been any fault at all, it lay in the fact that neither of them realized how much he had changed since his last trip to Nepal. And it was not until the police rang, an hour later, that the nightmare began.

The police refused to give much information over the phone, just that Richard had failed to stop at a crossing and a lorry had crashed into the side of his car. He was hurt and an ambulance had taken him to hospital, but, apart from advising Eva to try to get there as soon as possible, they said little more.

Amanda felt horrified and filled with despair, but, strangely enough, after the first shock had passed found she was able to take control. A wave of unsteadiness came and went, and she prepared to subdue her own fright in order to help Eva.

Eva was distraught. 'I should never have allowed him to go alone!' she kept repeating, her face white and full of regret.

Amanda did her best to reassure her, attempting to put on a brave front even while her heart was heavy with fear. There were things to be seen to before they got away, small things like Sam's biscuits to be topped up, and the kettle removed from the hotplate on the range. Thinking to distract Eva for a few minutes, she sent her upstairs for her outdoor things. 'I'd better ring for a taxi,' she said, exactly as Jason strode in through the front door.

'Amanda!' he exclaimed, his voice edged with a slight irritation. 'I said I would pick you up. Didn't you hear me arrive?'

'I'm sorry, Jason,' was all she could find to say as she stared at him blankly, not really seeing him as her stunned mind grappled with the problem of the taxi. To begin with she had quite forgotten they had only one car, which was now probably wrecked beyond repair, and the only available taxi would be the one which she had hired on that very first night during the storm. The driver would be sure to recognize her again! Yet it didn't seem possible that she should be worrying about this when it was imperative they got to hospital immediately. With determination she reached for the receiver, only to find with startled dismay Jason's hand on top of her own, stopping her.

'My dear girl,' he snapped, his fingers biting, 'before you go any further will you kindly tell me what's wrong? You look as if you'd seen a ghost.'

With another murmured apology she told him, for a moment letting her eyes rest on the dark height of him, renewing once more the feeling of security which the sight of him always seemed to give. 'So we have to get a taxi,' she finished flatly. 'Eva is shocked—she couldn't possibly travel any other way.'

For a split second the pressure of Jason's fingers tightened hurtfully. 'You were going to ring for a taxi,' he exploded softly, 'while all you had to do was get in touch with me?'

Amanda flinched as he released her trapped fingers. 'I'm afraid I didn't think about you—not after the police rang,' she said unevenly. 'In any case, you might have been busy.'

'The horse arrived,' he explained briefly. 'I intended to fetch you to have a look at her. Remember I did suggest it, and you agreed.'

While he spoke he was picking up her coat from where she had laid it on a nearby table. Helping her into it, he passed her a headscarf to tie around her hair. He didn't for the minute mention Richard at all. 'The weather this morning is definitely colder,' he remarked, his eyes keen on her numbed face. 'We could be getting more snow. You'd better keep warm. I know where you keep your drinks. I'll go and get you something while you get Eva downstairs, then we'll be off right away.'

It seemed to Amanda that from that moment Jason took charge. Afterwards she couldn't imagine how she would have managed without him. He had made Eva have a drink, and calmed her down by using, it seemed, just the right amount of firmness and sympathy. By the time they arrived at the hospital she had managed to pull herself together remarkably well. Jason's big car ate up the miles as it carried

144

them swiftly to Exeter.

Richard was gravely ill. He lay in a side-ward, holding on to life by a slender thread, and in spite of her newly found calm Eva was horrified and upset. Richard's head and right arm were bandaged and he was unconscious. She stood gazing down at him as if she couldn't really believe he was the same man for whom she had cooked bacon and eggs just a few hours earlier. Amanda forgot her own grief at the expression on her face. Eva was obviously devoted to her father, and deeply shocked by what had happened. In a rather futile attempt to comfort her, Amanda put an arm around her shoulders and drew her close, feeling a surge of new affection blending with her pity.

The nurse said that a doctor would see them immediately. Jason came with them, and Amanda noticed the way in which the white-clad nurse glanced at him with some appreciation. It was strange, Amanda thought, that she should notice this when her father was so gravely ill. With another apprehensive look at Richard's still figure she followed the others from the room.

The doctor was exceedingly kind but could tell them little more than what they had already guessed. Richard had sustained multiple injuries. The crash had been a bad one and he was very ill, but, eventually, there was every chance of a recovery, although to what extent it was as yet impossible to say.

'In many ways your husband is fortunate to be alive,' the man told Eva. 'He has escaped relatively lightly, taking everything into consideration. No one injury is in itself very serious; it's his general condition which I'm rather doubtful about. Has he been ill lately?'

Eva replied. 'Not ill exactly, doctor, but rather strange. Definitely not himself—tired, perhaps I should say . . .' A little helplessly she glanced at Amanda, who nodded her head.

'My father has been out in Nepal,' she explained, briefly. 'He's a biologist. He was in charge of an expedition. You may have heard of him.'

145

'Professor Trent?' The doctor's fair eyebrows rose. 'I've read many of his articles. He does good work, and he's just returned from Nepal, which could explain his symptoms very well. He's probably, unbeknown to himself, been suffering from exhaustion. Such pursuits can try a much younger man. When your husband recovers, Mrs Trent, I should advise you to keep him nearer home.'

It was reassuring that he didn't appear to doubt Richard's eventual recovery, but even so, Eva refused to leave her husband's bedside until he regained consciousness. Amanda stayed with her, extremely anxious herself about her father, in spite of what the doctor had said.

Jason, after making sure they had everything they needed, left to see the police and to sort out any official details. The accident had clearly been Richard's fault and, although the wagon involved and its driver were relatively unscathed, there would no doubt be some charge, even if only that of careless driving. The police took a dim view of those who apparently ignored the rules of the road completely. Richard's car, unfortunately, would never be a car again!

Some of this Jason related when he returned to the hospital, but not all. Eva thanked him, relieved to know that that side of things had been taken care of. It was late in the afternoon before Richard came around, and then only for a few minutes. But during that short time he did seem to recognize Eva and gain some comfort from knowing she was by his side. His head was swathed in bandages and the Sister told them that he had four stitches in his scalp and ten in his arm, together with bruised ribs. Until they were able to get him X-rayed it was impossible to assess the extent of any further damage.

'His colour is improving,' she said brightly, 'but we must wait and see.'

Later, Jason returned to Combe Farm to collect Eva's dog and take him to Merington. Amanda stayed behind with Eva so that they should both be near should Richard need them. Jason found them a very comfortable hotel near the hospital, each bedroom with its own bath and telephone. It seemed expensive, but Amanda was too shocked at the time to give that point much consideration. Not until afterwards did she learn that it was one of Jason's own, one of the three which he owned in Devonshire. She was even more dismayed when he refused to allow them to pay anything for the privilege of staying there. And when Eva accepted, thanking him with obvious gratitude, she remained silent, for the first time since she had known Eva annoyed with her.

'We don't want to be in Jason Meade's debt,' she reproached her later. 'We aren't yet reduced to having to beg, surely!'

Eva glanced quickly at Amanda's mutinous face as they set out for the hospital. 'We might have to do more than that if Richard doesn't recover completely. Besides,' she went on, with a slightly ironical smile, 'it's quite clear that Jason is paying you a lot of attention. I'm not quite blind, my dear. And I shouldn't want to do anything which might offend him in any way.'

Amanda gasped. They had stopped at a crossing, waiting for the lights to change to green, and she turned to Eva indignantly. 'You're jumping to all the wrong conclusions,' she began. 'Richard's illness . . .'

'Oh, come off it, darling,' Eva interrupted with a marked lack of finesse. 'Richard's illness hasn't made me oblivious to everything else. Jason might concern himself with those in trouble, but in this case I'm convinced there's more to it than meets the eye. However,' she conceded, 'apart from this, I did think it a good idea to keep on the right side of him. I'm always hoping that eventually he might agree to buy the river.'

'Which would mean an awful lot to you?' Amanda asked, her heart strangely heavy.

Eva nodded. The lights changed and they went across.

Richard's condition still gave rise to some anxiety and, although he improved daily, the outlook seemed far from reassuring. As the days went by it seemed quite clear that he would require much care and attention over the next few months and, at this stage, it was impossible to judge if he would ever work again as he used to. The doctor was still doubtful.

Another aspect filled Amanda with uneasiness. A telegram had been sent to Veronica, who sent word back that she would be over as soon as possible, just as soon as she could get away. She was, she said mysteriously, engaged in something very important, something which she alone could cope with, otherwise she would have caught the next plane. Somehow the prospect of seeing Veronica again didn't bring the comfort it ought to have done, and Amanda wondered why. Naturally Veronica would be worried about her father, it was quite normal that she should rush to his bedside. Yet something—something quite different, Amanda suspected, could be responsible for Veronica's visit. Richard might only be providing the excuse she'd been looking for.

Despite the fact that she knew her doubts to be unreasonable, Amanda found this inner apprehension almost unbearable and found small comfort in telling herself firmly to wait and see.

# CHAPTER NINE

For Amanda the next few days seemed haunted by a strange unreality, a feeling that much was to happen which could be momentous but nothing which she could in any way avoid. She tried to tell herself it was because she had nothing much to do, apart from visiting the hospital. Her nerves were merely playing with a too vivid imagination. The worst that could have happened had happened with Richard's accident. Fate could have nothing more traumatic in store for her than that.

Not until afterwards did she realize how foolish she had been not to take her intuition seriously. The blow fell when Jason asked her again to marry him. Over the past week she had been lulled by a sense of false security into thinking that he had changed his mind about her. That, for all Eva's teasing, his watchful vigilance, his concern for their comfort was prompted by a feeling of compassion, nothing more. It was disconcerting to find she had been completely wrong.

He arrived early one afternoon and asked her to stay behind while he drove Eva to the hospital. She would have liked to refuse, aware of a slight uneasiness, but something in his face silenced the words of protest before she could utter them. So she remained in the lounge until he returned. She sat in one of the darker corners, trying unhappily to relax, yet finding it impossible to even touch the drink which Jason had ordered for her before he left.

When he returned he ordered beer for himself from the usual subservient waiter and slumped down beside her. He stretched his long legs as if he was a trifle weary and, apart from saying he had delivered Eva safely, he didn't speak again until the man came back. He wasn't apparently in a hurry. Nor did Amanda make any attempt to find out what he had on his mind. Perhaps her ever active sixth sense warned her that what she was about to hear would be in no way welcome and she sought, if only by silence, to prolong the moment when he might explain.

She didn't have long to wait. 'I've arranged with Eva for you to spend the rest of the day at Merington,' he began coolly. 'But first we must talk.'

Amanda blinked, gazing at him uncertainly. He took too much upon himself! 'I can't leave Eva,' she retorted, feeling she was being organized. 'You know she needs me.'

'And you, my dear girl, need a break. Have you looked at yourself lately?' His glance stayed on her too slim figure, her huge shadowed eyes.

Amanda might have told him that her appearance couldn't altogether be put down to Richard's illness, but she knew better than to confess her innermost doubts and fears to Jason Meade. 'In a day or two,' she replied, looking away from him carefully, 'I expect to return to the farm. Someone ought to be there to keep the place aired. At this time of the year dampness soon creeps in. Eva is getting rather worried about it, especially as she thinks my father might be allowed home. As soon as I get back I'll come and collect Sam. I'll see your horse then.'

Jason muttered something impolite about horses beneath his breath. 'I'm not talking about horses, Amanda. And, as regards Combe Farm, Mrs Drew can pop in and do all that's necessary. You can see Sam this afternoon at Merington, but first, as I've already said, I want to talk to you.'

'What about?' Aware of a mounting nervousness, Amanda stared around her, looking anywhere but at his dark face. The lounge was empty. People, she supposed, rarely came to Exeter to sit in a hotel lounge, especially at this time of the year. She wished they did. Surrounded by people she might not have felt so conscious of Jason, might not have felt so certain that after she had listened to whatever he intended to say nothing would ever be quite the same again. She found herself swallowing some kind of primitive fear as his voice effectively jerked her to him.

He said smoothly, 'It might be just as well to start with

your father. You must know that in future he'll have to take medical advice and stay nearer home.'

Amanda relaxed slightly, although her slim fingers still gripped the edge of her chair. Perhaps he just wanted to discuss Richard. Slowly she nodded her head.

'You realize this will limit his activities?' There was a harder note in Jason's voice.

'Maybe he should have done this before now,' she murmured, not able to understand why Jason should be emphasizing the point.

'But he didn't.'

'No—he would never listen to reason. This accident, should he be otherwise all right, might prove a blessing in disguise.'

'Quite easily,' Jason agreed suavely. 'If he'd been blessed with a little more foresight. But as it is I gather he's always been a sight too independent. He has spent a great deal of his time and money on research unconnected with any specific job. Instead of sticking to a university career which would have supplied him with a suitable retirement pension, he could now find himself high and dry with barely enough to live on—certainly not enough to supply his immediate needs.'

'How on earth do you know all this?' Stung, although unable to deny the truth of what he said, Amanda rounded on him fiercely, two patches of pink on her cheeks lighting her face up indignantly. 'You must have been extra busy!'

'You could say that,' he drawled, not in the least disturbed by her anger, giving the impression that her words were wasted, like cotton-wool, without any impact. 'To satisfy your curiosity, my dear Amanda, a lot of this I've known for some time, and the other day Eva and I talked.'

'Talked?' Into a barely imperceptible pause she choked over the question.

'Don't worry,' he mocked. 'I don't think your step-mamma betrayed any secrets. Together we went over a few things which were worrying her. She might just as easily have consulted her bank manager or solicitor. I merely happened to be on hand and, taking everything into consideration, was probably the best person to turn to.'

Her voice was shaking. 'I'm still not with you . . .'

He grinned ironically at that. 'I don't think you are, but you must have some idea. You can't be an ostrich for ever, Amanda.'

His laughter, low though it was, inflamed her. Icily she said, 'You'd better try explaining.'

He looked at her sardonically. 'Hasn't it occurred to you that if Richard could sell his land and river his worries would be over? Definitely over in terms of hard cash.'

'And you're going to buy it?' she asked tautly.

'That depends.' He came very close to her, an intent look in his eyes.

'They don't have to depend on you, surely?' Amanda was suddenly furious—or frightened, she didn't know which. Suddenly she hated Jason for what she sensed was to come.

'Who else,' he reminded her, 'would be prepared to give more than what I'm offering? You'd have to look a long time, my dear. And you would also have to look a long time before finding anyone willing to buy the land without the house. And your father needs that house—especially now. It might almost kill him to leave it.'

'The neighbours?'

'Certainly none of your immediate neighbours are interested, even if they could afford it, which I doubt.'

She remembered how he had been confident of his ability to outbid another buyer to get the horse he fancied, and she knew a flare of resentment. 'And you could,' she taunted. 'How nice to have money!'

'You've said that before, Amanda. I warn you to be careful.'

Was there a threatening note in his voice? She took a deep gulp of air, feeling suddenly that she was drowning. Her pulse missed a beat, then continued painfully. 'You said it depends?' her mind backtracked uneasily.

He didn't keep her in suspense any longer. 'It depends whether you'll marry me or not,' he said.

'Marry you!' Her eyes widened and her voice trailed off on the last syllable as she swallowed abruptly. She felt herself go white.

His tone was hard and goading. 'Don't pretend to be surprised. I've asked you before.'

'I do remember, Mr Meade,' she replied tersely, straightening her shoulders.

'Well, then?' he pointed out, his eyes with the glint of steel in them not at all her idea of a man proposing.

Rather desperately Amanda lowered her gaze and looked down at an empty ash tray, as if expecting it to provide inspiration. 'You make it sound like another of your business propositions!'

'Maybe because you choose to look at it that way,' he suggested.

She glanced at him briefly, shaking her head, breaking away from his sardonic stare, not knowing why she couldn't bear the way he looked at her. Her heart thumped and her mouth felt dry. She might have been something he had seen in a shop window. Something he fancied, but not for any particular reason. But surely there had to be a reason?

She asked stubbornly, 'What other way would you expect me to look at it? I'm merely applying my own interpretation. People don't marry for no reason whatsoever.'

'I have a reason all right,' he countered, his eyes narrowing. 'You can take it I feel a certain attraction. Besides, I could do with a wife. Maybe I feel a need to settle down and have a family. A son and heir has some appeal to a man in my position.'

Amanda felt her cheeks grow hot as a strange perverse excitement ran through her. He taunted, but his words defeated her against her will. Jason was an attractive man; she accepted that. His features were rugged, his mouth determined. Sitting beside her in a blue town suit, his darkness accentuated by his crisp white collar, he had the power just by looking at her to make her heart beat faster. And

153

because she loved him she could be in danger of grabbing what crumbs he offered, gratefully. It could be wiser to refuse him—if she had any choice?

Perversely she strove to keep her voice even, to ignore his last remarks to some degree. He made it quite plain what would be expected of her! He didn't believe in beating about the bush—Well, for that matter, neither did she. 'If I agree to what you ask,' she began recklessly, 'you will pay my father exactly what he wants for what he has to sell?'

'Every penny,' he agreed coolly. 'He'll have my cheque right away. Just as soon as you're wearing my engagement ring.'

'And if not . . .?'

A crooked smile played about his mouth, not quite reaching his eyes. 'I don't think we need consider that point, Amanda. You wouldn't care to have me mention the week you spent with me during the storm. If not your parents, there are others who would undoubtedly be interested. Perhaps you would enjoy a local scandal?'

The definite threat in his voice made her go cold all over, even while a wild fury shook her. If she ever doubted he was adamant she didn't now. It seemed he would stop at nothing in order to have his own way. 'You're detestable!' she spluttered.

'Merely stating facts.' His tone grew detached, as if the conversation was beginning to bore him. 'I wouldn't be a good business man if I didn't know when to apply a little pressure.'

Her lip caught painfully between small white teeth. Jason meant what he said, she knew it. Helplessly she looked away from his hard green gaze. She didn't really believe that he would broadcast that week of indiscretion, but he might tell Richard and Eva, and that she could never bear! Dully she heard herself saying, 'Okay, you win,' and wished the hardness in her voice could be reflected in her heart.

'You won't regret it,' the quirk at the side of his mouth

154

belied the formality of his words. 'You don't feel particularly gracious, but that will come later. You must be glad for your father's sake, at least.'

Her eyes gleamed like ice crystals. 'I mustn't think of myself!'

'Let's say that for the moment I'll do your thinking for you,' he responded, still taunting, his eyes alive on her rebellious face. 'I'm quite aware of a degree of immaturity so far as your emotions are concerned, but I don't think you're afraid of marriage and all it involves, Amanda.'

She stopped abruptly at the hard edge in his voice. She dared not fling another remark at him, yet all of a sudden she didn't want to. Nothing she said could help her at this moment. Later perhaps her turn would come. In the meantime she must exercise patience. It could do no harm. Better this than that Jason should guess how much his indifference hurt.

Demurely, and apparently with a proper confusion, her lashes swept down on to her cheeks. 'I've always thought of marrying one day,' she admitted.

'Of course you have!' Now his tones matched her own, although his expression remained dark and immobile; curiously watchful. If he was pleased with himself it only showed in the gleam of his eyes as they rested on her small, delicate features. 'Like most women you like making a great ado about nothing, but we must get this thing settled right away.'

From his pocket he drew a box and opened it reflectively. Nerves strung to breaking point, Amanda saw it contained a ring—a beautiful, sparkling diamond engagement ring, seemingly a clear indication that he hadn't doubted her ultimate surrender.

'Yours,' Jason said smoothly, and with some satisfaction, as she stared wordlessly. From the arm of her chair he took her hand, slipping the ring on to her third finger. 'Every girl should have diamonds,' he said firmly, as he lifted her hand to his lips.

Her hand moved convulsively in his and his grip tightened with a fine flare to his nostrils as his head came up. 'I hope you like it?'

Appreciate it, he means, Amanda thought a trifle wildly as feeling surged from the touch of his lips. The ring gleamed on her finger, sparkling against the light—a thing of beauty, worth probably, she hazarded, more money than she had ever possessed. Dazed, her glance shifted from the ring to his face, meeting his eyes. 'It's very nice,' she said slowly.

'Very nice!' For a second his dark eyebrows rose impatiently as he flicked her hand on which the huge diamond flashed ostentatiously. Then he sighed with a shrug of his broad shoulders. 'You're not exactly enthusiastic.'

'This is hardly the place——' she began, then stopped uncertainly. How could she tell him that she wished he had waited until they had arrived at Merington? To become engaged in a hotel lounge was so impersonal, in fact totally inhibiting with a member of the staff hovering, if discreetly, in the background. Of course, if she was rash enough to point this out, he might only retort that theirs was no ordinary engagement, that the usual betrothal endearments belonged to an intimacy they didn't share.

Flushed with the confusion of her thoughts, Amanda jumped quickly to her feet. 'I'd rather go now, please, if you don't mind.' Her former sentence she left unfinished.

Jason rose abruptly, only a split second behind her. His hand dropped to her shoulder, gripping, bruising as if perfectly aware of all the things she left unsaid. His expression was a compound of no-nonsense and alertness. 'On our way to Merington we'll call at the hospital,' he told her. 'And remember, my darling, you're supposed to be in love with me. I shouldn't like your father to get the wrong impression.'

The only impression Amanda noticed at the hospital was one of delight. Eva threw her arms around them, and Richard, with transparent relief which he made no attempt to hide, wished them well. As they left, Amanda reflected bitterly on how much she appeared to have risen in her father's estimation—especially when Jason openly promised him a cheque in the morning.

At Merington she accompanied Jason to the stables, still feeling she was living in some dream world quite divorced from reality, not even the heavy ring on her finger giving her dream much substance. Jason showed her his new mare, a horse full of singular grace and beauty, and for a while Amanda wandered, finding pleasure in renewing old acquaintances amongst the other animals in their stalls.

The Drews offered their congratulations, Tom Drew saying very little but Mrs Drew adding that she hoped they would both be very happy. On the way there Amanda had been anxious about the Drews and not really relieved when Jason had told her to leave the Drews to him.

'I've told them all they need to know,' he had assured her. 'You don't have to worry. The Drews have an excellent position, one which I hardly think they would be keen to jeopardize in a hurry, as I've told you before.'

All the same, Amanda decided unhappily, they must be thinking it a very unusual situation, and she had found herself wishing, as she had done so often lately, that she could have met Jason under more normal circumstances.

But, in spite of her doubts, the momentous day continued as if everything was exactly as it should be. Jason opened a bottle of champagne, insisting that they all had a drink. Tom Drew, mellowing after his second glass, beamed, and Mrs Drew smiled in her usual friendly fashion and asked Amanda about her father. She was pleased, she said, to hear he was so much better, and that the little dog, Sam, would no doubt be delighted when he was home again. Of course he was no bother.

She was pleasantly talkative, but never once indicated by a word or glance that Miranda Smith had ever existed. It was both comforting and disquieting, if two such emotions could be felt at the same time. Jason, however, appeared to have no such qualms, and Amanda was silently aware that he would have little sympathy with her uneasiness.

157

Later in the evening, after they had eaten the very good dinner which Mrs Drew had prepared, he said. 'We'll be married in about two weeks—just as soon as I can arrange it. Your father will be home and I'll see to it that Eva has plenty of help.'

Amanda looked at him, attempting to think coherently. His expression was steady but enigmatical, despite the straightforward statement. Two weeks! Her pulse raced, then settled to an erratic beat. She couldn't possibly marry him so soon. And why should he be in such a hurry?—it wasn't as though he was madly in love! If he had been she might have been tempted to agree, but although she did realise that eventually she would have to go through with it, a one-sided union had little appeal.

'I'm afraid I would need more time,' she declared woodenly.

He sighed deeply as if praying for patience. 'You were falling over yourself to find a job only a week or two ago!'

Hastily she lowered her lashes. 'That isn't quite the same thing.'

'You can say that again!' Amanda could feel he was appraising her as she stared down at her hands. His voice was determined. 'But you were prepared to start work immediately.'

'I don't think I was,' she retaliated, 'and the same thing applies now.'

'Surely, Amanda,' he protested, 'you're not comparing marriage to me with a job? Although,' his voice teased, 'I do expect to be in command—in more ways than one.'

A quiver of fear and something else—some totally unpredictable feeling, ran through her. She had no illusions about marriage with Jason. He wouldn't want to know anything about the emancipation of women, not in his own home. He would expect to rule the roost, and he would expect her to be suitably amenable. There might be much, she acknowledged, that she would receive in return, but what she really longed for he would deny her. And her life would be wholly barren without his love. A slight sickness washed over her, making her cold and shivery, and her heart ached.

Ruthlessly he took her silence for acquiescence, refusing to apply any other construction. He studied her a little unnervingly, yet there seemed a new gentleness about him, an unwillingness to throw the sheer weight of his more dominant personality against her less robust strength.

'Come here, Amanda,' he said quietly, and when reluctantly she joined him on the huge leather settee before the fire he put his arms around her, drawing her softly against him. 'Stop worrying, girl,' he smiled. 'Leave everything to me. Perhaps we're doing things the wrong way around. Don't you know you haven't kissed me since we became engaged?'

Their eyes met as she stared at him, startled. A little mutiny stirred. 'You don't expect me to anticipate your every mood? I wasn't to know what was expected of me!'

Jason's grip tightened. His smile deepened to low laughter as he surveyed her flushed face. 'I should like you to be clear on that point at least.'

He drew her closer and kissed her, very softly on her lips, but not in quite the same way as he had done previously. There seemed to be about his arms and mouth a tenderness which had been missing on those other occasions. Amanda felt surprise, and a little disappointment touch her. Yet, after a moment, she found this new approach equally satisfying. Her own lips responded to the insidious restraint of his, and she found herself curling up against him, her body soft and boneless, her hands creeping around his wide waist, yielding herself to the hard masculinity of him. When he lifted his head she had a dreamy, half satisfied look on her face as she stirred against his shoulder.

Together they lingered until it grew late, watching the firelight. They didn't speak, and Amanda felt a new drowsiness overtake her, subtly dangerous but utterly irresistible. Jason's hands, she found, could charm as surely as his lips ever did . . . Together they stayed and watched the firelight, hearing only the sound of crackling wood and November wind against the window. And with the same wind came strange sounds in the old chimney, a vague suggestion of long-lost, long-dead travellers, still wandering the moor, still pleading to be in. Or was it Jason's lips against her cheek with their soft murmurings which almost, if not quite, succeeded in sending her to sleep?

Almost . . .! The man, as if sensing the danger Amanda wasn't wholly aware of, put her gently away from him and rose to his feet. 'I'm taking you home now, my darling,' he said abruptly, but almost as if he meant the endearment.

For one long, heart-stopping moment, Amanda almost thought that he did!

After four whole days Amanda began to feel that, given time, all would be well with her world. It wasn't a definite feeling so much as a nebulous one. Something instinctive, like knowing it was spring before the calendar said so; like knowing the flowers would bloom because a bud was on the tree. It was a lightening of spirits which made her realize she was young and in love, even if not entirely satisfactorily.

If Jason had the air of a man prepared to bide his time she pretended not to notice. For reasons, perhaps as he had stated, he wanted to marry her, and had been ready to resort to blackmail to achieve his ends. But as the days went by none of this seemed to register any more. He didn't ask her again to Merington, although she knew he intended they should live there, and after they were married she could, he said, refurbish in any way she liked. If it came to her imperceptibly that there were advantages in being a wealthy man's fiancée, it struck her forcibly what it would mean to be his wife.

But if he was completely attentive and willing to humour her in every other way, he remained adamant about the date of their wedding, and Amanda's half-hearted attempts to make him change his mind met with little success.

'A trousseau isn't necessary,' he told her firmly. 'After we're married you can shop. I'll buy you anything you like. On our honeymoon we stop at Paris first.'

He was ready, she thought wistfully, to give her luxuries when all she longed for was one word of love. The pattern was all too familiar. As he had said, he needed a wife and she would adorn his table and be rewarded accordingly. Apart from the odd moments of sexual attraction her feelings were not returned. Amanda's face softened and saddened. It was like being near to heaven but separated by a thin glass wall. A flick of humiliation touched her but couldn't altogether kill a quiver of hope. Maybe, if she was patient, it might all come right? In the meantime there seemed little else she could do but fall in with his wishes. Half a loaf could be better than no bread. Just to live with Jason might be better than not having him at all.

Eva said, 'I think we shall all be worn out before your wedding day, darling. What with Richard's accident, your marriage, and Christmas so near! I almost envy your father his inability to move.'

About Richard this wasn't strictly true, but Amanda knew what she meant and sympathized. There was so much to do.

Richard was home. He had been discharged sooner than they had expected, and while able to move around the house unaided, still needed much care and attention. Still, it was lovely to have him back, and his continuing delight over the now healthy state of his bank balance more than compensated Amanda for her heartache.

Altogether the few days following her visit to Merington passed pleasantly enough. There was nothing whatsoever to prepare her for the chaos which was to come.

Veronica arrived one stormy December night when the wind blew so hard they scarcely heard her taxi. They hadn't known when to expect her and were quite startled when she walked in the door. Eva and Richard were sitting by the fire. Amanda was making after dinner coffee in the kitchen.

She had been to Exeter with Jason. While Richard had been there in hospital there had been little time to explore the beautiful old city. Jason and she hadn't exactly done this, this afternoon. They had just wandered around, because, as he said, the winter days were really too short and dull for proper sightseeing. He had shown her the cathedral with its two famous Norman towers, and the magnificent west front with the carved figures. And inside he had pointed out the fifty-nine-foot-high Bishop's Throne, the minstrel's gallery and the astronomical clock in the north transept. Just opposite the cathedral, in the Close, he had taken her to see Mol's coffee house, a building where Elizabethan sea-captains used to drink. There were many other places to see, he had told her—the University, museums and art galleries; the River Exe, only five minutes' walk from the High Street, but he had a meeting that evening with some of his hotel managers and didn't want to be late. It seemed to Amanda that he made a point of being busy in the evenings, and in a fit of pique had asked him why.

'You wouldn't appreciate the answer to that one,' he had laughed, as he had kissed her goodbye.

But only gently. As the percolator bubbled she thought of the way he kissed her nowadays with a strange, unsatisfied yearning. He didn't see her in the evenings; he kept her at arm's length when he did take her out. Could he, she wondered, with a decided drooping of spirits, be regretting his hasty proposal? It was only when she considered his new tenderness, her own growing sense of happiness, that she got on with the coffee, telling herself not to be so silly.

Then in came Veronica, sweeping aside Amanda's newly acquired tranquillity. She was beautifully dressed in the latest fashion and hadn't yet discarded the smart little fur hat which sat smoothly on top of her sleek dark head. The slight twist of her lips could have passed for a smile. 'That coffee smells super,' she said, surveying the steaming percolator greedily. 'I'm ravenous, as I've just been telling Eva. I don't think I've eaten much all day.'

For no reason she could think of Amanda's heart sank. It was as if she and Veronica had only parted yesterday, and on the best of terms—instead of the reverse. Uncertainly she gazed at her sister, trying to gauge her mood. Veronica, she knew from experience, was rarely as she appeared to be.

'Have you nothing to say, darling?' Veronica prompted.

'Oh, yes, of course. I'm sorry . . .' Amanda exclaimed. 'You startled me, that's all. For a moment I thought I was seeing a ghost.'

'Or wishing I was one?'

'Why, no, certainly not. Don't be silly. We were expecting you.' Amanda quivered, unable to define the cool note in Veronica's voice.

But before she could utter another word Eva appeared, almost, it seemed, to the rescue. 'Were you as surprised as I was to see Veronica, darling?' She addressed Amanda, her air protective, making it quite clear she was prepared to stand between the two sisters if need be.

Amanda nodded, forcing herself to smile. She asked Veronica, deliberately casual, 'How did you manage to get here at this time of night?'

Veronica shrugged. 'I got a taxi, sweetie-pie. The man was very obliging. He told me he hadn't been to Combe Farm since the recent storm when he dropped someone off in the snow.'

Colour surged beneath Amanda's skin, and she knew Veronica was aware of it as she turned away abruptly. 'You must be relieved to see Daddy so much better,' she stammered.

Veronica hadn't missed the colour. She shrugged again, but her eyes were keen. 'Richard was always lucky,' she said lightly. 'I should have been surprised to find him otherwise than greatly improved.'

Why then did you come? Amanda almost cried, restraining herself just in time. Veronica would only consider her impertinent. Instead, she said stoically, 'Daddy will be pleased to have you here.' Yet as she spoke she wondered if this would still be true. Hadn't Richard told her himself that he had almost quarrelled with Veronica, although none of them had ever known him to bear a grudge. Still, there was always a first time, although for Veronica's sake in this instance, she hoped not.

From a distance, it seemed, she heard Eva saying that Richard was always pleased to see any of his family. If there was just the faintest hint of reproach in her voice at Veronica's somewhat critical demeanour, then Veronica chose not to notice. 'How is Herman?' Eva went on, filling a small gap of silence. 'He hasn't come over with you?'

'He did,' Veronica frowned. 'As a matter of fact he's been returned to London for a week or two by the Embassy. This is why I didn't come sooner—I felt I couldn't leave him on his own.'

An admirable sentiment, if one which didn't ring quite true. Not as Veronica said it—she seemed curiously evasive. Amanda bit her lip nervously, suddenly finding herself reluctant to mention Herman's name. He still left a nasty taste in her mouth, a reminder of something she would rather forget.

Eva smiled quickly, sensing undercurrents. She turned to Veronica. 'You won't have heard yet about Amanda's engagement. We didn't send you a wire in case you were on your way.'

'Engagement?' Veronica looked surprised. 'Why, she's only been home a few weeks!'

Veronica talked over Amanda's head, almost as if she didn't exist, and Amanda remembered with some apprehension that her sister had been friendly with Jason herself! More than friendly according to Eva and, even if she hadn't wanted him herself, Veronica was not prone to be generous with her cast-offs.

'Amanda has been home long enough,' Eva said firmly. 'She's now engaged to Jason Meade. I'm sure you'll be pleased about it. Richard and I are delighted.'

Veronica was not! 'Jason Meade! Good heavens—you must be joking!' She stared at Eva with patent dislike, her face a study of startled emotions. 'Why, she doesn't even know him!'

'Your sister does happen to be standing behind you,'

Eva pointed out sharply. 'And she is wearing Jason's ring. Why don't you look and see for yourself?'

Slowly, feeling rather like a puppet on a string, Amanda lifted her hand. The faint touch of triumph in Eva's voice blending unhappily with Veronica's ill-concealed antagonism. On her finger Jason's diamond seemed to flash with a challenging brightness.

Amanda heard Veronica's breath catch in her throat, a raw kind of sound, and her colour heightened. After that first incredulous glance she didn't look at the ring again. Her eyes, returning to Amanda's pale face, held a glittering kind of anger. 'Jason's too old for you,' she cried coldly.

'He's only in his thirties,' Eva pointed out when Amanda refused to answer.

'Just!' Veronica retorted.

'You exaggerate,' Eva rejoined, but with something in her manner which must have warned Veronica she was going too far. Eva prided herself on her tolerance, but she would only put up with so much.

Amanda, making a supreme effort, stirred, attempting to shake off a peculiar lethargy. Veronica always had this effect, but she couldn't go on sheltering behind Eva. 'I suppose,' she said, 'this is rather sudden, but these things happen.'

'I should be interested to know how,' Veronica replied enigmatically, her expression proclaiming louder than words her opinion of Amanda's naïve little speech. 'However,' she added, with apparent caution, 'I suppose you know your own business best. When is the wedding to be?'

This last seemed tacked on merely as an afterthought, without any real conviction that such an event was ever likely to take place. 'Before Christmas,' Amanda retorted, more sharply than she otherwise might have done.

'So it's lovely that you and Herman will be here,' Eva put in sweetly.

Amanda was well aware of Eva's protective instincts, but knew it was time she fought her own battles. Her skirmish with Veronica, before Veronica had gone to America, seemed to have given her courage. Now she tilted her chin and said with cool dignity, 'As Eva has just said, it will be lovely to have you. Jason and I are to be married at the end of next week, which should work in with your plans very well.'

Afterwards Amanda realized that her new composure had not achieved the desired effect. Veronica, while still looking annoyed, had obviously been restrained by some inbred caution. Her lips stretching in the slightest of smiles, she had quickly left the room, murmuring abruptly that she was going back to talk to Richard. Eva, after throwing Amanda a wry grimace, had promptly followed.

At this rate Eva would be worn out long before the wedding day, Amanda thought distractedly. Veronica's tongue could be cruel as well as kind, and Eva was quite aware of it. That was just it, Amanda decided, as she set about preparing Veronica a light supper. Just when Veronica said something spiteful, and one was beginning to hate her, she cleverly reversed the trend by saying something nice. But such an atmosphere was not comfortable to live in, and Amanda, in an enlightened moment, breathed a gentle sigh of relief at having escaped in time. Whatever happened, she vowed she would never again live with Veronica, no matter what anyone might say. If only she could get through the next few days without mishap, all might be well.

But in spite of her optimism the vindictive expression on Veronica's face continued to make her uneasy—this, and a growing awareness that Jason had meant something in Veronica's life, whether she was prepared to admit it or not. Amanda sighed a little as she picked up the percolator and a plate of ham sandwiches, placing them on a tray. Would it be unsisterly, she wondered, to wish that Veronica, like bad weather, had never arrived? Or again, like bad weather, that she might simply go away!

# CHAPTER TEN

Of late when Amanda had woken in the mornings she had known, before full consciousness came, a feeling of happy anticipation. This morning there was nothing but a curious sense of foreboding, some vague notion that all was not well with her world and that she would be better to go back to sleep. This feeling of apprehension, she realized, must have something to do with Veronica being here.

The night before, just as she had been getting into bed, Veronica had come to her room and talked. She had chatted lightly about living in Washington, D.C. She didn't really care for it, she had said, although it had possibilities. Herman was out a lot, she didn't see much of him. If Amanda had been there she wouldn't have been so very lonely. And so on . . .

To all this Amanda had listened, simulating interest, her wariness in no way lulled by Veronica's easy manner. Veronica, however, never once mentioned Jason or, even casually, Amanda's engagement. She had only asked why Amanda had disappeared so completely in London after she had left the flat.

'I tried to find you,' she explained with a reproachful yawn, 'but you seemed to have disappeared. I looked everywhere—I even rang Merington in case you'd come down here. But of course you hadn't.'

Once again that evening Amanda had found herself flushing and unable to hide the hot colour in her cheeks because of the bright light above her head. And again, although Veronica's eyes narrowed, she had made no comment. Not even when Amanda rejoined with nervous uncertainty, 'I stayed in a hotel.'

'Really, darling,' Veronica had drawled, 'you might have told me. It was such a silly little quarrel, after all.' Her tone of voice had clearly indicated that she was quite prepared to forgive and forget the whole incident if Amanda was willing to do the same. But in spite of a feeling of relief, Amanda had been glad when at last Veronica had said goodnight and retired to her own bed. Her whole body felt taut, in no way relaxed as she was struck by the sudden conviction that things were to happen over which she might have little control.

Now she stirred with a dismal kind of sigh, then sitting up quickly, glanced at her watch, seeing to her horror that it was well after nine o'clock. She had over-slept, which came of talking into the early hours. All the hustle and activities of the last few days topped by Veronica's arrival must have proved exhausting. Not, Amanda chided herself as she hurriedly scrambled out of bed and threw on some clothes, that this was any excuse. She ought to have been up ages ago helping Eva. The daily help wasn't coming this morning and there would be a lot to do.

A few minutes later she stood in the kitchen pouring herself a cup of tea. Eva walked in, a bright smile on her face as she saw Amanda.

'Richard insisted on getting up early,' she said. 'He heard Veronica leave and I think it disturbed him.'

'Veronica?' Startled, Amanda shot a quick glance at Eva as she put down the pot. 'You mean . . .'

'Oh, nothing like that—she hasn't gone for good. She's only gone to Ashburton for cigarettes. She forgot to bring a supply, and I'm afraid I couldn't help, and I knew no one else could either.'

'Oh, yes. I see . . .' Amanda turned away, tidying the kitchen table while her tea cooled. Veronica had only gone for cigarettes, certainly nothing which might account for the quiver of apprehension which shot through her now. Yet it was rather strange that Veronica should dash off at this hour of the day. Amanda never could remember her smoking much in the mornings.

Eva was shrugging her elegantly clad shoulders, almost as if she guessed something of what her younger stepdaughter was thinking. 'Being in the country makes your sister restless. She often went off like this when she stayed before. The cigarettes might only be an excuse.'

Which ought to have been comforting but somehow was not, and did little to dispel the nervousness in Amanda's heart. Nor did it help when Veronica rang later to say she had met an old friend and wouldn't be home for lunch. And when this call was followed almost immediately by one from Jason, who said abruptly that he wanted to see her right away, Amanda stared at the receiver with anxious dismay. That something was wrong seemed obvious from his tone of voice. Rather wearily she smoothed her hot forehead with impatient fingers. Maybe it was nothing? Perhaps his meeting the previous evening with his directors hadn't gone according to plan? Such things did happen, especially nowadays when so many companies were running into trouble. But before she could give more than her brief assent the line went dead, and she was left holding the receiver with the distinct feeling that her fingers had been burnt.

Jason had said he would send Tom Drew over for her in the car, but in spite of his request for haste it was after one before Tom arrived, just as she was beginning to think he wasn't coming at all.

She hadn't bothered to dress, but kept on a pair of blue slacks, pulling a pullover over a thin blouse. Jason, she thought, applying a little optimism, might be busy in the stables and permit her to help.

The car arrived, Tom apologising for being late. Nothing had gone according to plan that morning, he grumbled, he would be behind all day. On top of this Mr Jason had been in a foul mood—'Begging your pardon, miss,' he said.

Glancing at him uncertainly, Amanda made no reply. His reference to Jason's mood was not encouraging, but it probably had to do with the stables, not herself. Tom told her that he was taking Mrs Drew into town to do some Christmas shopping after he dropped Amanda.

'She says there won't be anything left if we don't get there soon,' he grinned, if not very enthusiastically, and

Amanda smiled back. But her smile faded for no reason that she could think of when he added, 'Of course when Mr Jason is away on his honeymoon I won't be able to leave the place, so he suggested I went this afternoon.'

Mrs Drew was waiting on the doorstep, smartly dressed for her shopping expedition. When the car drew up, Amanda got out and she got in. 'I expect you'll find Mr Jason in the library,' she said cheerfully. 'He told me to tell you he would be there.'

Amanda gazed for a moment after the swiftly disappearing car, her winged brows drawn, renewed dread in her heart. It wasn't like Jason to be so offhand, of late he had been more than attentive. But perhaps she was getting spoilt! She couldn't expect him to be at her beck and call all the time. Besides, in some ways their relationship wasn't exactly a normal one. Jason, for all his attentiveness, had never pretended to be in love with her. Still, it didn't do to dwell too much on that. Brushing the tumbled hair from her eyes with an impatient sigh, she turned and ran quickly into the house.

As Mrs Drew had told her she found Jason in the library. He stood with his back to the fire, facing her as she came in through the door. There was a half empty glass in his hand, and something about his expression pulled her up short.

'Come in, Amanda,' he invited politely, but his voice was so stony that the impact hurt, driving the colour from her wind-flushed cheeks, lighting her eyes with apprehension.

'Jason ...' she began uncertainly, as she took another step into the room.

But before she could go on he cut her short, his eyes ruthless on her nervous face. 'I had Veronica here this morning,' he stated abruptly, 'and she enlightened me about several things. I thought it was time we had a frank talk, you and I.' His tone was bleak and uncompromising, blending darkly with the winter's afternoon.

'Veronica!' Amanda was stunned. Her voice came in a horrified whisper, and her face paled. 'But she's only just arrived! She came last night.'

'I'm quite aware of that. Sit down, Amanda.' His mouth tightened grimly. He had the appearance of a man holding himself on a tight leash, only the habits of a lifetime restraining his more primitive impulses. 'I'll get you a drink,' he added coldly, without reassurance. 'Perhaps you're going to need it!'

Helplessly, Amanda sank into the nearest chair, clutching at her scattered senses. Numbly she stared at him. Even before Jason said anything more she knew what was to come, and she felt herself tremble. Veronica had obviously, in a fit of jealous rage, told him about Herman. She must have intended doing so all along—she probably had been unable to help herself. The cigarettes had only provided an excuse to leave the farm so early. In that instance Amanda knew intense regret, a despairing remorse that she hadn't told Jason herself, yet in retrospect it hadn't seemed feasible. She hadn't been sure that Jason would understand, and she hadn't wanted to be the cause of any ill feeling between the two men. She had reasoned that if they were to be brothers-in-law, the less said the better. Veronica, too, she had concluded, would much rather forget the whole thing. It wasn't as if anything had actually happened.

Or had she—Amanda considered her own motives with a painful honesty—merely been using these evasions as a means of avoiding something unpleasant, something which in telling might only have reflected badly on herself? It was confusing, this turmoil of uncertainty. Unhappily she continued to stare at Jason's broad back. Small wonder he had made no attempt to kiss her as she came in, and was pouring himself another liberal measure of whisky. And from the hardness of his expression it seemed clear that he had allowed himself time to think things over, to form his already obvious conclusions, none of which seemed favourably disposed towards his fiancée.

Amanda shuddered, dragging her eyes away from his silk-clad shoulders to stare about her with half-seeing eyes.

The afternoon was rapidly darkening, the grey clouds outside bringing a spatter of rain against the window. Inside the room was dim, the heavy curtains half drawn to keep out the cold. But it was warm in the room, in spite of a fire which only smouldered, as if reflecting the mood of the man who stood beside it. He had given her a drink, setting it down on the table by her side without asking as he usually did, what she preferred, or even if she had wanted anything at all. All of which seemed a clear indication that he was prepared to treat her with contempt.

For the first time since she had arrived Amanda felt a stir of anger. Her conscience was clear, whatever he thought! He had no right to judge her without even waiting to hear her side of the story. Her rounded chin lifted, indignation forcing a sparkle to her eyes where a second ago she had felt the prickle of defenceless tears. 'You were about to say?' she prompted coolly.

He drank off half his whisky in one quick swig before he drew nearer, placing his glass on the table beside her own. As he stared down at her his face was grim. 'What I'm about to say, Amanda, might not make pleasant hearing.'

She waited, not breathing.

'Veronica said——' his voice hardened, 'that you'd been having some sort of affair with Herman, which was why you took off in such an almighty hurry and came down here— after she'd almost caught you in the act.'

'And you believed her?' Amanda's breath released added a trembling emphasis to her words.

He ignored this. 'She seems to have a good idea as to where you spent the following days. Maybe you told her— proud, no doubt, of the habit you seem to have acquired of collecting scalps.'

'I didn't tell her any such thing!' Furiously Amanda jumped to her feet, her face scarlet. 'What do you take me for!'

'I'm beginning to wonder! She found you and Herman in the bathroom,' his voice was cold with distaste. 'What do you expect me to make of that?'

Blankly she stared up at him, her dark blue eyes almost black with emotion. 'That would surely depend on the amount of trust you have in me, but already you appear to believe the worst.'

'Oh, come off it, Amanda,' he laughed ruthlessly. 'All this innocent pretence seems a bit dated. We live in a fairly permissive society. It's beginning to be the accepted thing. The mistake I made was in thinking you different. We could have wasted a lot of time.'

The ironical coldness in his voice didn't deceive her for one minute. She sensed that he wanted to hurt her, hurt her badly. She could have told him that already she was mortally wounded because of his lost faith, of the way in which he condemned her. And because of this she could have cried.

With some effort she controlled herself—after all, a girl must hang on to her pride. She went back to his second last sentence, saying tersely, 'And because Veronica chose to tell you some tale, a complete fabrication, you assume I'm not?'

'It's not your fault I put you on a pedestal,' he said belligerently.

'Well, it was flattering while it lasted! Actually,' her voice cracked, 'I never put you on one at all.'

'You could try explaining?' His eyes glittered with a fury to match her own.

Yet there was also a dangerous calm about him which ought to have warned her—which might have done if she hadn't been past caution of any kind. Her voice rose. 'You encourage Veronica hoping to get the river on the cheap. She was half in love with you. Probably she married Herman on the rebound, although it was nice of you to allow the story that she'd turned you down.'

His eyes were icy, for a moment frightening her into silence. 'This is none of your business,' he grated, his jaw tight. 'And it won't help your cause to throw insults in my direction. The fact remains—when you stayed here you

173

stayed under false pretences. You weren't what you made yourself out to be.'

Amanda heard herself asking shrilly, 'Whatever do you mean?' Her whole body felt hot and trembling and her voice somehow out of control.

His mouth twisted with curt contempt. 'Oh, I was the fool, my dear, I'm quite ready to admit it. I put myself out to protect your reputation from the big bad world outside. I believed that if I treated you kindly you might come to care for me. I imagined you were innocent, when in reality you had little virtue left . . .'

Unable to stop herself, Amanda shot her hand out, making contact with his scornful face. Aghast, she stared at the spreading red mark on the granite carved cheek, yet she felt no real regret. There was only hatred in her heart and a primitive desire to hurt more.

It was then that his arms went out, as with a muttered oath he dragged her to him, hurting with his hard, virile strength as he caught and held her soft, pliant body to his own. Desperately she tried to escape as her head fell back against his shoulder. She was aware of his barely controlled violence, aware that the only thought in his heart was of revenge. If she had ever regretted the gentleness of his recent kisses she thought wistfully of them now, in the split second before his lips crushed down on hers and she knew no more.

He kissed her possessively, his lips claiming hers with a sensual abandonment, without restraint, intent it seemed on arousing a flame of desire within her to match his own. And as response came, yearning became uncontrollable passion, a flame and surge of ecstasy transcending place and time.

He lifted her, sweeping her up in his arms and carrying her out through the door, up the wide staircase to his room. She had never been here before. He threw her down on the bed and she felt herself pinned beneath the weight of his heavy body. She had no idea how lovely she looked with her hair loosened and dishevelled, her tremulous lips, the high flush on her soft white skin. She heard Jason's breath drawn sharply above the thudding beat of her heart. And then his lips were on hers again, his hands sliding to the warm skin on her back, up and around. She was lost, submerged, floating in a world where time ceased to count.

Then, with a suddenness that was like a douche of cold water, he lifted his mouth from her face, wrenching her arms from where they clung tightly around his neck and leaving her lying crushed against the white sheets. He halted just one moment beside the door, his back towards her, not apparently willing to spare her another glance. 'Any time you're ready you can go,' he said curtly. 'You can leave my ring or keep it, whichever you choose. There seems little sense in prolonging an engagement which has become meaningless.'

Long after he had gone Amanda lay as if unable to move. She was limp, numbed, depleted by a soaring rapture. She felt weak, emptied of emotion. Her lips hurt, and her body where his hands had touched, yet she scarcely noticed. Little by little she was beginning to realise how much Jason meant to her, and unable to visualise the devastation of her life without him. She was even ready to confess, if only to herself, that whatever he might have demanded of her a few minutes ago she would have been more than willing to give. She had no defences to stop him, nor had she wanted to, her total submission must have been obvious in the responsive warmth of her own lips and arms as he had held her to him.

Why—why, she moaned almost aloud, burying her hot face against the pillow, had he left her so abruptly? Why, when his opinion of her was so low, hadn't he finished what he had so ruthlessly begun? From the pillow came the faint scent of the cologne he used and, for an impulsive moment, she clasped it to her, closing her tear-wet eyes, imagining it was the man.

Then, just as suddenly as he had done, she slid off the bed. Hurriedly groping for her pullover and shoes, she swiftly left the room, tearing down the stairs out of the front door as if the devil himself was after her. A new panic mixed up with a sense of shame seemed to propel her unconsciously, a sure knowledge that if she stayed any longer she would find herself searching for Jason, begging him with ignominious humiliation to give her another chance. Whatever the heartache, no matter how bleak the future might appear to be, she must never stoop so low as that.

There was no one around as she went out. Of course the Drews were in town, she had forgotten. She saw now that Jason must have deliberately arranged it, and bitterness welled with relief. He had thought of everything, his actions obviously premeditated to ensure that no one would witness his final act of revenge. But that which hurt most was not his anger or even his subsequent rejection, but the fact that he had so utterly believed everything Veronica had told him.

Almost four miles lay between Merington and Combe Farm, but Amanda, having walked it before, didn't hesitate now. There was, after all, no alternative. She had no other means of getting home, being willing to brave the elements rather than beg Jason for a lift, even if she had the courage to face him. And to wait until the Drews returned was unthinkable. The wind buffeted her, whipping her long hair behind her as she ran, and the rain came down, draining over her face, but somehow she didn't feel the discomfort. If she hurried she might just catch the evening train to London. She made plans. Tomorrow she would get in touch with the Randalls. They were keen to have her back any time—she had had a letter. She had only, they had said, to let them know—they would arrange everything. It was a means of escape and she meant to take it. In a very few days she could be out of the country, and away from Jason for ever.

Veronica hadn't returned when she reached the farm, and Amanda was relieved. But this also meant there was no car available, so she rang for a taxi. The man promised to be there in half an hour. She ran straight upstairs. Richard was having a nap, something for which she was thankful, but she met Eva on the landing.

Eva considered her stepdaughter's drenched state with startled eyes. 'Where on earth have you been, darling?' she exclaimed. 'Where is Jason?'

'At Merington,' Amanda explained briefly, while throwing off her wet clothes. 'Look, darling,' she said, and there was a trembling note in her voice, 'this is going to be a shock, but our engagement is off. Which reminds me—I'd like you to give Jason this.' Hastily she pulled off her ring, almost thrusting it into Eva's hand. 'He asked me to leave it, but somehow I forgot.'

Aghast, Eva looked from the glittering ring to Amanda's still, white face, her own face stunned. 'I just refuse to believe it!' she gasped.

Amanda carefully ignored this. 'I'm going to London,' she went on, as if Eva had never spoken. 'I've arranged for a taxi, it won't be long. I shall probably go back to the Randalls, so you don't need to worry. I shall miss you, but of course Daddy should be all right now. And the agreement about the river is completed and signed up. Jason couldn't do anything about that, even if he should want to.'

'Amanda!' Eva half shouted, alarmed by the wild rush of words. With some exasperation she continued as Amanda fell silent, 'I'm not bothered about the river, or whether your father and I can manage. Will you tell me, please, what's happened? You come in half drowned and as white as a sheet and expect me not to ask questions. Surely, all things taken into consideration, I have some right to know?'

Amanda was busy zipping herself into a pair of dry trousers, prior to throwing a few things into a suitcase. She half turned, glancing at Eva with heavy weariness. 'There's nothing really to tell, darling. We found out we weren't suited, that's all.'

Eva frowned, but only slightly. Her eyes still retained a flicker of hope. 'Only a lovers' quarrel, perhaps?'

'Never that!' Amanda sounded so vehement that Eva started, shocked, her face crumpling suddenly as if she was about to cry.

177

About to lock her suitcase, Amanda left it to come over and put her arms around her. 'Eva dear,' she said, 'I'm sorry, truly I am—about you, the preparations and—well, just everything, but please, can't we leave it at that? None of this was ever any fault of yours. Don't ever think so.'

Something, something tense in Amanda's pale, exhausted face must have warned Eva against saying any more. After a moment she composed herself, asking instead, 'Where will you be staying in London? Have you made any plans? Don't you think it would be better to wait a few days before rushing off like this?'

Emphatically Amanda shook her head. She thought of her father's old cousin who used to keep house. 'I'll probably stay with Rebecca,' she replied. 'At least for tonight. She doesn't have much room, but I can always sleep on a cushion. But please, Eva, I want you to promise not to mention this to anyone. Not,' she added bitterly, 'that anyone is likely to inquire, but just in case.'

It was only when she was sitting in the taxi on the way to the station that she realised that neither of them had spoken of Veronica. Deliberately she had tried not to think of Veronica herself and, of course, Eva would have no idea what Veronica had been up to. Amanda frowned; she had yet to try and work it out. Apart from jealousy what other reason could Veronica have had for acting as she had? In going to see Jason, in telling him a completely fictitious story, she had intentionally or otherwise spoilt any chance of happiness her sister might have hoped for. Even with some basis for such a tale, much of it, as she had tried to explain to Jason, was complete fabrication, and Veronica was well aware of it. But surely, somewhere, there must have been something, something beyond her own knowledge, Amanda decided with a sense of growing misery. Something in which Jason had been personally involved. She remembered his anger, his refusal to talk about it, and shuddered. Yet in spite of her unhappiness she was glad she hadn't said anything to Eva or Richard. Veronica would return to the farm and be company for them, helping to tide them over her own departure and no one need be any the wiser. Besides, what use to any girl was a man without even a modicum of trust?

It was almost eight when she arrived at Paddington and, for a few minutes after leaving the train, stood gazing about her, only half conscious of the hurrying crowds. Leaving Combe Farm had proved a greater wrench than she could ever have imagined it would be, and she tried unsuccessfully to put it from her mind. But it was one thing, she discovered, to decide what to do, and quite another to put those same conclusions into practice. But the fact remained that Jason didn't want her. He considered she had made a fool of him, and deliberately planned his revenge. Why then was she finding it difficult to realise she had had a fortunate escape? To be married to a man with so little faith, who was prepared to doubt one's every word, could only lead to misery!

In time, Amanda assured herself, she would forget. Must forget! It would be impossible to live for ever with such intolerable pain; with such a feeling of loneliness, such an inner conviction that she might never love again. Never in the same way! This afternoon Jason, by some devious trick of fate, might have left her whole, but she knew, with aching certainty, that he had spoiled her for any other man.

A wave of weariness overtook her as, with some effort, she left the station, and a nervous headache began to niggle at her temples and over her eyes. She knew she had had about enough, knew she was almost physically as well as mentally exhausted, and for this one night, at any rate, not fit to start looking for a hotel. She had better stick to her former plan and visit Rebecca. Rebecca might grumble, but she couldn't possibly turn her away.

She hailed a taxi. It seemed to be becoming a habit. It was also probably wildly extravagant considering the rather doubtful state of her finances, but right at that moment, tired, and with the chill December wind penetrating her thin coat, she felt she couldn't face the journey by any other means.

Rebecca answered the door herself and appeared in no way surprised to see who stood on her doorstep. A half smile curved her thin mouth, but it was quite something in one who seldom smiled at all. Amanda was positively startled by it. It surprised her still more when Rebecca stepped back, beckoning her by a wave of her hand to come inside. 'I suppose you'll be after a bed for the night,' she commented, as she closed the door and fixed the lock before ushering Amanda through into her sitting-room.

'Not a bed, exactly,' Amanda, reverting to a habit from childhood, smiled pleadingly. 'A cushion would do, Rebecca, in fact I'd rather sleep on your settee, if you wouldn't mind?' Somehow the thought of a bed did things to her pulse, accelerating the beat of her heart uncomfortably.

'Well, just as you like,' the old woman was saying as Amanda followed her in. 'It's either that or sharing a room with my friend, and she went to bed an hour ago. She hasn't been feeling so good today.'

'I'll stick with the settee,' Amanda answered with a wry smile. Then, politely, 'I'm sorry about your friend.'

'Her own fault,' Rebecca grumbled. 'She went out without a hat. She deserves all she gets.' Thus disposed of, the friend was not mentioned again. With some semblance of hospitality Rebecca stirred the fire, removed Amanda's coat and went out to make some tea. 'I'll be back in a minute,' she said.

Amanda waited, sinking into a chair with a sigh of relief. Rebecca fussed a lot, but then she always had done, and she couldn't be expected to change now.

She was almost asleep when Rebecca returned with a tray containing two cups and a plate of biscuits. 'I suppose,' she said, as she poured out, 'you're here to do some shopping for your wedding?'

'Wedding!' Amanda stared at her bent head, aghast. But of course, Eva had naturally sent an invitation. This surely explained why Rebecca's mood was mellow.

'Yes, your wedding, dear.' Impatiently Rebecca looked up. 'Although you must know I shan't be able to come. The journey would be too much for me, especially at this time of year. I posted a letter to your dear stepmamma only this afternoon.'

With a quick gulp Amanda glanced for a moment into the fire, not able to find the right words with which to tell Rebecca of her broken engagement, but before she could speak Rebecca continued with a nod of approval.

'I believe your fiancé is a wealthy man. And you're a very wise girl to settle for an Englishman. Not like your sister and her American. Little wonder she's lonely, over there on her own.'

For the first time in her life, so far as Amanda could recall, she was one up on Veronica in Rebecca's estimation. Not that it mattered, she told herself, looking at Rebecca helplessly. It wouldn't last long. She would have to confess that the wedding was off. It was then she decided to wait until morning. She would tell Rebecca before she went. She couldn't bear all the questions, the recriminations which would result from such news.

So she just smiled again gently, murmured something, which obviously carried no weight, about Veronica being happy and listened a while, while Rebecca rambled on. But she felt grateful when a few minutes later Rebecca heaved herself to her feet, announcing without apology that she was going to bed, and would advise Amanda to do the same.

'And don't try to waken me, my dear,' she warned. 'I take a sleeping pill and sleep like a log.'

Which was just as well, Amanda mused later when she first heard the sharp rap on the outer door. It was almost midnight. Too tired and numb to feel really worried, she glanced at the clock. Maybe someone had lost his way or needed help? It must be a man—it could even be a policeman at this time of night. Anxiously she tumbled off the settee. After Rebecca had gone to bed she hadn't bothered to undress, but had sat in a dispirited sort of daze, staring into the fire, seeing in the flames a film-like sequence of the past weeks. She hadn't wanted to see, not even in her mind's eye, but the pictures had kept floating by, each one more

181

sombre than the other. The happiness, the heartache, had all been there, but more condemning than all, her own folly.

The knock on the door, though startling, proved a welcome release. The second knock, when it came, propelled her into immediate action. Rebecca had taken a pill, but that was enough to waken the dead!

In the small hallway she switched on the light and called who was there, all in one breath. Better to be safe than sorry!

'Amanda, for God's sake open this door before I knock it down or freeze to the step!'

It was Jason. For one terror-stricken moment Amanda stopped short, then, driven by a compulsion stronger than herself, she did as she was told, with fingers which shook so much that the simple task took much longer than it ought to have done. 'Jason,' she said through the awful constriction in her throat, and could say no more.

He stepped inside, not waiting a further invitation, his face grim as his eyes flashed over her, as he grasped her arm. 'Are you alone?' he asked harshly. 'Can we talk?' And as she nodded, still speechless, the door closed significantly behind him.

'Rebecca has gone to bed,' she managed, as he almost thrust her back into the dimly lit sitting room with fingers which were none too gentle.

'Long may she stay there,' he ground out, sweeping her around to face him, his terse glance penetrating her white face, her huge shadowed eyes, the tremor he could feel running through her slight body. 'Thank heavens I've found you!' he muttered, pulling her into his arms.

It wasn't until a long time later that Amanda began to be conscious once again of time. All she was aware of was Jason's voice, murmuring that he loved her, that he couldn't live without her, as he cradled her against him, kissing her cheeks, her eyes, her throat before at last her lips, his own as warm and passionate as she could ever wish for. It was an avalanche of feeling, a dream materializing,

182

just having him there, being able to hold and feel him. It was a flare of emotion that left her clinging to him blindly so that she would have fallen if he had not held her.

'Jason,' she pleaded on a trembling breath against his mouth, 'please tell me why you are here?'

'I thought I'd done that already, my darling.' His lips trailed fire over her cheek.

'You haven't,' she muttered somewhat incoherently. Impossible to think clearly as his arms pressed her closer, as his lips explored the throbbing pulse at the base of her throat.

Reluctantly, it seemed, he raised his head. 'I have only an urgent desire to make love to you,' he said. 'Heaven after the sheer hell of the last few hours! You'll have to forgive me, Amanda, there's no other way.'

'How do you mean?' she asked, her heart in her blue eyes. 'You didn't want to see me again.'

'Amanda!' Taut pressure lines formed beside his chiselled mouth. His hands slid away from her body, catching her wrists, still holding her. 'After you'd gone I think I went berserk. I'm not too proud to admit it. You don't know how badly I wanted you. It took me about a couple of hours to come to my senses, to realise exactly how much I loved you, but by the time I got to the farm you were well on your way. Eva would only tell me that you were going to London. I managed to wheedle this address out of Richard, but had no idea if you would be here. Richard wasn't sure. Anyway, long before I reached the station your train had gone, and I was left to cool my heels, waiting for the next one.'

'But surely——' she protested, but he cut her off.

'Just listen,' he said with a little of his old authority, touching a finger to the tiny frown between her fine dark brows. 'I was there, pacing the station with fine ill humour, when who should get off an incoming train but Herman. I'd been cursing myself for listening to the story which Veronica had told me, for refusing to believe you when all my instincts told me you were telling the truth. In any case, my darling, I was past caring. I only wanted to find you, to find out if you cared at all, if you would forgive me. Nothing else was important. Then along came Allen. I could cheerfully have knocked him down!'

Amanda's eyes stayed on his dark face. 'But you didn't!' she breathed in some despair.

'I felt like it,' Jason returned dryly. 'I even took a step towards him, only to change my mind. I wasn't going to speak to him, but he spotted me before I could disappear. I don't know your brother-in-law all that well, Amanda, but well enough to be able to see that he'd been imbibing too freely on the train. I decided, rather reluctantly, that I'd better sober him up a bit, otherwise your parents might get a shock if he arrived at Combe Farm the way he was.'

'Then what happened?'

'Nothing much,' Jason said tersely. 'Actually he wasn't as bad as I'd thought, or perhaps the black coffee did the trick. He was soon okay, but he started to talk and I couldn't shut him up. He said he'd been recalled unexpectedly, and was rushing down to Devon to spend the weekend with Veronica and her family before they went. Veronica wouldn't hear of him going back alone. It was then that he started telling me about Veronica's jealous little ways. He had a vague idea, he said, that Veronica's sister was at the farm, and he'd been drinking to bolster himself up. Then it all came out, in one long self-pitying ramble, and I don't think he had the faintest notion that I knew you at all. He confessed to having surprised you in your bathrobe—a kind of a joke, he said, which had just fizzled out. How you were about to brain him with a candlestick when Veronica appeared. How he hadn't even managed to get near you, but how Veronica had refused to listen to reason. When I told him, my darling, that he'd been talking about my fiancée, you should have seen his face!'

'Jason,' unable to think coherently, Amanda was shaking, 'were you ever in love with Veronica yourself?'

'No, never that!' he grunted decisively. 'She started

coming to Merington quite a lot. I rather enjoyed her company until she began to get too possessive, but completely without justification.'

'Eva thought you quarrelled because of the river.'

'The river,' he shook his dark head emphatically, 'had nothing to do with it. I didn't explain why I didn't buy it to anyone. You see, I didn't really want it. I intend to put most of my hotels on the market. I'll keep the property which I have abroad, and Merington, and concentrate, I think, on breeding and training horses, as I used to. If you'll help me, Amanda, and you'd better say yes!'

'Darling,' Amanda murmured some time later as if the thought had just occurred, 'but you did buy the river, after all?'

'Of course I did, young woman,' his hand curved her soft chin possessively. 'Everything seemed weighted against me. I had some fixed idea that I was about to lose you. I had to stop that happening, and the river seemed all I had to hold over your head.'

'When you only needed yourself.' The colour came beneath her skin as she evaded his fingers and buried her head against his chest. 'I loved you so much, Jason, almost at once, and you never guessed.'

'Amanda!' Urgently his hand returned to her throat, lifting her mouth to his and there was a long silence as his lips crushed hers again, drowning her words. She was almost without breath as his head lifted, his heavy eyes dwelling with some satisfaction on her flower-like face. 'I tried to restrain myself, young woman. I thought if I treated you gently you might come to care for me. You had me well nigh distracted, that night when you first came to Merington, soaked with snow and rain. You were unconscious, but I thought I'd never seen anything so lovely, so desirable. At first, I confess, it was just plain desire—until you ran away. I could cheerfully have murdered you, my darling, but it was then that I began to realise I must have you for my wife. I've never asked anyone before, Amanda, not even you. Not in the right way, with love in my heart, no bribes, no threats, nothing else.'

'Jason!' she smiled up at him, aware with everything within her that what he said was true. There was no barrier any more, and nothing between herself and paradise but this man who would walk with her. 'Darling,' she murmured, her smile fading even as she teased him, 'you can have me for the rest of my life, if that won't be too long.'

'And beyond,' he threatened, his eyes going over her with soft menace as he pulled her closer. 'Nobody or nothing will ever trouble you again, I'll see to that. But you'll never escape me, and you'd better not try!'

'Who would want to?' she protested before his lips stopped all speech, blotting out the firelight, all conscious reality, leaving only his arms and a wild sweet singing through her heart.

# Have you missed any of these best-selling Harlequin Romances?

# By popular demand... to help complete your collection of Harlequin Romances

**100 titles listed on the following pages...**

# Harlequin Reissues

# Harlequin Reissues

# Harlequin Reissues

# Harlequin Reissues

# Complete and mail this coupon today!

Harlequin Reader Service
MPO Box 707
Niagara Falls, NY 14302

In Canada:
Harlequin Reader Service
Stratford, Ontario N5A 6W4

Please send me the following Harlequin Romances. I am enclosing my check or money order for 75¢ per novel ordered, plus 25¢ to cover postage and handling.

| | | | | |
|---|---|---|---|---|
| ☐ 901 | ☐ 1006 | ☐ 1354 | ☐ 1400 | ☐ 1505 |
| ☐ 904 | ☐ 1011 | ☐ 1356 | ☐ 1401 | ☐ 1506 |
| ☐ 905 | ☐ 1013 | ☐ 1357 | ☐ 1402 | ☐ 1507 |
| ☐ 907 | ☐ 1019 | ☐ 1358 | ☐ 1403 | ☐ 1509 |
| ☐ 911 | ☐ 1025 | ☐ 1360 | ☐ 1404 | ☐ 1513 |
| ☐ 913 | ☐ 1026 | ☐ 1362 | ☒ 1406 | ☐ 1516 |
| ☐ 915 | ☐ 1030 | ☐ 1364 | ☐ 1407 | ☐ 1517 |
| ☐ 918 | ☐ 1036 | ☐ 1366 | ☐ 1410 | ☐ 1519 |
| ☐ 920 | ☐ 1044 | ☐ 1369 | ☐ 1411 | ☐ 1523 |
| ☐ 924 | ☐ 1048 | ☐ 1370 | ☐ 1412 | ☐ 1524 |
| ☐ 925 | ☐ 1107 | ☐ 1373 | ☐ 1413 | ☐ 1527 |
| ☐ 927 | ☐ 1109 | ☐ 1374 | ☐ 1414 | ☐ 1534 |
| ☐ 931 | ☐ 1117 | ☐ 1376 | ☐ 1415 | ☐ 1536 |
| ☐ 932 | ☐ 1122 | ☐ 1377 | ☐ 1417 | ☐ 1537 |
| ☐ 967 | ☐ 1125 | ☐ 1378 | ☐ 1418 | ☐ 1538 |
| ☐ 973 | ☐ 1136 | ☐ 1379 | ☐ 1419 | ☐ 1539 |
| ☐ 977 | ☐ 1228 | ☐ 1381 | ☐ 1421 | ☐ 1541 |
| ☐ 985 | ☐ 1230 | ☐ 1386 | ☐ 1422 | ☐ 1543 |
| ☐ 1004 | ☐ 1266 | ☐ 1387 | ☐ 1425 | ☐ 1544 |
| ☐ 1005 | ☐ 1274 | ☐ 1389 | ☐ 1429 | ☐ 1546 |

Number of novels checked _____ @ 75¢ each = $_____

Postage and handling                                    $_____.25

                                            TOTAL    $_____

NAME _____
                        (Please print)

ADDRESS _____

CITY _____

STATE/PROV. _____ ZIP/POSTAL CODE _____

MOR 2022